IN BLACK AND WHITE

A NOVEL

BY

MARYANN DIORIO

TopNotch Press

A Division of MaryAnn Diorio Books

Merchantville, NJ

IN BLACK AND WHITE
by MaryAnn Diorio

Published by TopNotch Press
A Division of MaryAnn Diorio Books
PO Box 1185
Merchantville, NJ 08109

Publisher's Note: This is a work of fiction. Names, characters, places, and incidents either are the product of the author's imagination or are used fictitiously. Any resemblance or similarities to actual persons living or dead, business establishments, events, or locales is entirely coincidental.

Scriptures marked KJV are taken from the King James Version of the Bible.

Softcover Edition: ISBN: 978-0-930037-53-6
Electronic Edition: ISBN: 978-0-930037-54-3

Library of Congress Control Number: 2019904658

While the author has made every effort to provide accurate telephone numbers and Internet addresses at the time of publication, neither the publisher nor the author assumes any responsibility for errors or for changes that occur after publication. Further, the publisher and author do not have any control over and do not assume any responsibility for author or third-party websites or their content.

Cover Design: Lisa Vento Hainline

Editor: Leslie Peterson

Praise for the Fiction of MaryAnn Diorio

The Madonna of Pisano

"From the first couple of pages my emotions were pushed into chaos. I kept wondering at how easy it is for people to believe a lie and allow doctrine to be their truth…. This is one beautiful story that makes Christ the Redeemer shine so brightly."
~ *Reader of Fiction*

"Excellent characters, dramatic plot. Beautifully written, giving wonderful feeling for the setting in place and time. Emotionally intense situations, satisfying resolution. Among the two or three best novels I have read this year. Highly recommended."
~ *Dr. Donn Taylor, Novelist and Retired Professor of Literature*

A Sicilian Farewell

"Such lovely writing—and an even lovelier story! Author MaryAnn Diorio takes her readers on a courageous journey, from the ancient romance of the Old Country to the perils and possibilities of the New Country. Well-developed characters and a story that will stay with you long after you've finished this enjoyable read."
~ *Kathi Macias, Award-Winning Author*

Surrender to Love

"I enjoyed reading *Surrender to Love* by MaryAnn Diorio. It was a short story that packed a powerful punch. Anyone who has ever experienced loss in their life, in any form, can automatically relate to the feelings of Teresa and Marcos in this book. In addition, there were three characters, each of whom experienced significant loss—but each from a different perspective; this brings even more depth to the book. It showcases how, despite knowing "what to do," it's not always

easy to tell your heart to do what your head knows it should. And that saying goodbye can feel like a betrayal of sorts…letting go of the old is more than just head knowledge—it has to come from the heart, a full surrender."
~ *Cheri Swalwell, Book Fun Magazine*

A Christmas Homecoming

Winner of the Silver Medal for E-Book Fiction in the 2015 Illumination Book Awards Contest sponsored by the Jenkins Group. "This short story is a wonderful way to start the Christmas season. It is a story full of human emotion and the struggles this life can challenge us with. The lesson throughout the story is that all things are possible through God's grace. This is a 'feel good' story that lifts the spirits and keeps you encouraging the main character to persevere and not give up. It is a great book for a short respite from our busy lives."
~ *Kimberly T. Ferland, Reader of Fiction*

"Well-woven. If only all stories made me sit on the edge of my seat, unsure of the outcome, but desperate for a good conclusion for the characters!"
~ *Sarah E. Johnson, Poet*

"A great Christian read. A powerful short story packed full of love, hope, heartbreak and a strong message on forgiveness."
~ *Jerron, Reader of Fiction*

*To my Awesome Heavenly Father
Who gave me this story of His heart …*

and

To all those who have been affected by prejudice of any kind …

In Black and White
by MaryAnn Diorio

Why black or white?
Why look at skin?
What will it take
to stop the sin
of stigmatizing God's creation
with unjust discrimination?

Why is it that
we fail to see
the truth that love
is color-free,
that hatred only
blinds the heart
and keeps both black
and white apart?

Why not proclaim
we are the same
in joy and laughter
grief and pain?
Why not look past
the outer skin
to find the spirit
deep within?

Oh, would that we
would rise above
the pettiness of
gross self-love,
and look beyond
the outer man
to find the brother
deep within.

In Black and White

Chapter 1

Philadelphia, Pennsylvania, 1959

The bold-print newspaper announcement of a Ghanaian art exhibit at the nearby Philadelphia Museum of Art caught Tori Pendola's eye. Anything related to art always caught her eye. Art had a unique way of soothing the deep-seated feelings of rejection that had haunted her life ever since, as a twelve-year-old child, she'd overheard her father complain to his best friend that she had been an accident.

An *accident?*

The word had thrown her heart into a tailspin. The angry tone of voice with which Pop had spoken it still blared in her ears, like the scraping of fingernails across a chalkboard. He might as well have said *unwanted.* It would have been more truthful.

She stifled the searing memory and, as always in times of emotional pain, she turned to art. It was her solace. Her refuge.

An escape from suffering.

Immersing herself in art helped her forget the dull ache that constantly gnawed at her heart. The dread-filled feeling that no one would ever want her. That rejection and loneliness would be her lot in life.

How she longed—needed—to know she was worth something to someone! That she was accepted despite her flaws and loved without condition.

She picked up the newspaper from the coffee table and turned toward her younger sister. "Anna, look at this! We have to go!"

Anna raised her eyes from her copy of *Cry the Beloved Country*, the novel that was still shaking the post-World War II world eleven years after its publication. "Go where?"

Newspaper in hand, Tori approached her sister and pointed to the advertisement. "It's an exhibit of Ghanaian art, right here in Philadelphia at the Museum of Art."

Anna scanned the newspaper. "Looks interesting."

"Only 'interesting'? It's fascinating!"

Anna chuckled. "Well, of course it's fascinating to you. You're the artist. But, to me? Well, let's just say I have other things that interest me more."

Tori gave Anna a charming smile. "Am I one of them?"

Anna laughed. "What do you mean?"

"I mean, will you go with me to the exhibit?"

Anna put her book down on the sofa. "Yes, dear sister. I will go with you." She smiled. "If I decide to pay attention instead of dozing off, I might even learn something."

Tori bent over and gave Anna a kiss on the head. "You're such a lovely little sister."

"Yes." Anna sighed. "I always let you have your own way."

Tori slapped her playfully on the arm.

Anna picked up her book. "So, when is this exhibit?"

"Actually, it launches tomorrow evening in celebration of Veterans Day with a lecture by a famous expert on Ghanaian art. My professor mentioned it in class yesterday and suggested we attend."

"Oh, so I've signed up for a lecture as well?"

Tori sat down next to Anna. "Only if you want to, of course."

Anna leveled her eyes with Tori's. "Tori, you have always been the persuasive older sister. But, I must confess, going along with your crazy ideas has always improved my life in some way in the long run."

"Why is this a crazy idea?"

"Because Ghanaian art is probably the most random thing you could have asked me about." She laughed before sobering. "In any case, it's 'crazy' because it has nothing to do with my more immediate concerns—like helping Pop. Mom suggested I help relieve him of some of the pressures of running the business. I'd been thinking of getting some extra work done tomorrow evening, but I think it can wait for another day."

Tori pondered Anna's words. Their father was getting up in years. He would be approaching his sixty-eighth birthday in a few short months, having fathered both of them late in life. He would have retired long ago but for the recession that had struck the American economy in the mid-fifties. Now that things were looking up economically in the country, he might reconsider retiring if he had someone to take over the family business.

Anna seemed to be that someone. At twenty-two, she had an acute business sense, was highly organized, and competent beyond her years. She'd taken after their father and was perfectly suited to run the business.

Tori, on the other hand, was allergic to what she considered the boring life of the business world. To working in an office and doing the same thing day in and day out. She wanted adventure. Excitement.

True love.

A love that was not conditional. A love that accepted her for who she was, flaws and all. A love that didn't require her to perform in order to be worthy of it.

Not Pop's kind of love.

She sighed. Would she ever be good enough for him? Would she ever measure up to his standards of excellence?

Would he ever love her just because she was his daughter?

Tori's gaze fell on her sister. Anna was the favored one. Their father had wanted Anna. Not that Tori was jealous of her sister. No, Tori was only sad Pop didn't love her in the same unconditional way he loved Anna. To Pop, Anna could do no wrong. Anna was the compliant one, never opposing him. Always agreeing with him. No wonder Anna had a better relationship with their father than Tori had.

Anna interrupted Tori's thoughts. "So, tell me more about this exhibit."

"Well, I don't know much more than you, except that African art is increasing in popularity."

"Why?"

"It has something to do with the growing realization that the art of non-Western cultures should not be judged by the values of Western art."

Anna yawned. "Well, I'll leave the philosophizing to you, my dear sister. It's time for me to fix dinner. Mom will be home soon from her ladies' club meeting and asked me to have the meal ready by the time she gets here."

While Tori deeply loved her sister, Anna was the pragmatist of the two of them, and Tori was ever the idealist. This difference in personality had made for some sharp arguments between them over the years, but it was also the glue that cemented their relationship. In the long run, opposites did attract. Tori and Anna were proof of that.

While Anna prepared dinner, Tori headed to her desk to get in a few more minutes of study for her midterm exams. The end of the semester was fast approaching, and she had to do well if she wanted to graduate with the rest of her class and please Pop at the same time. He continually reminded her he'd paid a pretty penny to send her to an Ivy League school, so she'd better produce a good return on his investment. After all, it wasn't every daughter of a small businessman who got to go to Penn. Talk about pressure!

She was competing with students from all over the world. Penn's Master of Arts program in Art History was considered one of the finest anywhere, and she was privileged to be a part of it. Yet, the stress of it all sometimes overwhelmed her. If only her father weren't hovering over her, measuring her success. If only she could rest in the knowledge that she didn't have to earn his approval by getting good grades.

If only Pop loved her unconditionally.

Tori sat down in the straight-backed chair at her bedroom desk and gazed out the window. Large drops of rain splattered against the pane, while dark-gray clouds melted into night. Here and there, house lights in her Italian neighborhood turned on as families prepared for another cold, rainy November evening.

She sighed. The demands of her studies were getting to her. She needed the break that tomorrow night's lecture would bring.

Redirecting her focus to the notes before her, she renewed her resolve to do something great with her life. She'd make a difference in the world. She'd touch people's lives with her art.

If for no other reason than to prove to Pop that even an "accident" could be worthy of his love.

* * * *

Jebuni Kalitsi exited the shuttle bus that ran from his University of Pennsylvania classroom building to the dormitory that housed foreign graduate students. At twenty-six, he was one of a handful of African exchange students who'd been admitted to Penn's prestigious School of Economics. Son of a tribal chieftain, he'd been sent to the United States by his father to learn the principles of Western capitalism that would help free his beloved Ghana from economic and social bondage upon his succession to the chieftaincy.

A succession of which he didn't feel at all worthy.

Large drops of rain fell on Jebuni's head while lightning flashed through the gray evening sky. The distant rumbling of thunder and the rising wind sent chills through his veins. He tensed. The same signs had preceded that fateful day. The day that had changed the course of his entire life ten years earlier.

Lightning. Thunder.

Wind.

He shuddered, stifling the tormenting guilt that had plagued him ever since, eating at his soul. Ripping it to shreds.

Maybe if he could bury the guilt, it would go away.

But, after ten years, it still hadn't faded. Instead, it had only intensified. Would it ever leave him?

A blast of wind blew across his face, sending a chill through his bones. The Philadelphia climate was a far cry from the hot, tropical temperatures of his native Ghana. He lifted his coat collar close around his neck and blew into his hands in a vain attempt to warm them. Even leather gloves didn't dissipate the chill.

He braced himself against the threatening storm. Just as the downpour began, he reached his dorm building. The lounge at the main entrance was nearly empty, except for a few students from South Africa and India who chatted excitedly while the evening news blared on a TV set in the background: "In a tragic turn of events, a fishing boat sank off the coast of Maine today, resulting in the death of twelve passengers."

Jebuni's blood turned to ice. The horrific, recurring memory flashed across the screen of his mind, as it had countless times during the past ten years. Why had he insisted that Kofi go on that fishing trip when his best friend had been reluctant to go? Could Jebuni have done more to save him?

Why had Jebuni survived while Kofi hadn't?

Pushing down the painful memory yet again, Jebuni waved at the students and made his way up to the third-floor apartment he shared with his roommate from Nigeria, Kelechi Adebayo, a student in Penn's School of Law.

Kelechi greeted him warmly. "Hey, man! It's about time you got home. I'm starving."

Jebuni laughed. "So, why didn't you cook for both of us?"

"Are you crazy, man? You know I can't even boil water."

"Then learn, my friend. Learn! Otherwise, one day when I've returned to Ghana, you will starve to death."

"When you leave, I will find myself a good wife to cook for me." He winked.

"But until then?"

"Until then, I will depend on you to be my personal chef."

Jebuni slapped Kelechi on the back and then proceeded to the table where the day's newspaper lay open. "What's in the news today?"

"Not much. The usual concern about communism's encroachment on the world. So, what else is new?"

Jebuni drew the newspaper toward himself and scanned the two-page spread. The word *Ghanaian* in large print caught his eye: *Ghanaian Art Exhibit and Lecture at the Philadelphia Museum of Art, Wednesday night, November 11th, 7:00 p.m. Free admission.*

His eyes widened. "Hey, roomie! Do you want to go to a lecture on Ghanaian art?"

"If it were Nigerian art, I might say 'yes.' But I'd better study for my midterm exams. They're coming up in a week's time."

Jebuni feigned surprise. "You mean you refuse to support Mother Africa?"

"I need to support Law Student Kelechi right now, or Papa Kelechi will revoke my stipend."

"Fine, then. I'll go myself. I'm so homesick that even an exhibit on Ghanaian art will encourage me."

"Or make you even more homesick."

Kelechi had a point. But missing Ghana as much as he did, Jebuni pushed the comment aside. Any connection with his homeland was better than no connection at all.

Nearly two years had passed since he'd left his native land to study in the States. With a bachelor's degree in history under his belt from Oxford University, he'd opted to spend another two years earning his master's degree in economics. Upon graduation at the end of the current academic year, he'd take himself and his degrees back to Ghana to spend the rest of his life there.

Jebuni folded the newspaper and went into the kitchen to cook up a meal. The refrigerator revealed a dozen eggs, a half loaf of bread, and a few apples.

He shouted to Kelechi. "How about a fried egg sandwich with an apple for dessert?"

"I've had better, but it will do."

As he fried the eggs, Jebuni's mind rushed back to the days of his childhood when his mother would make him *hausa koko*, a millet porridge flavored with sugar, milk, and ground nuts. How he loved it! And how he loved even more his mama who made it! He missed her. She was his staunchest supporter, his greatest fan. In her eyes, Jebuni could do no wrong.

It had been Mama who'd tried to comfort him during the tormenting days after Kofi's drowning. During those sleepless nights when he'd tossed and turned, weeping and railing with guilt and remorse, she'd sat beside him for hours, praying for peace to come upon him. It was Mama who'd encouraged him to go abroad, hoping that distance would bring healing to his wounded soul.

But distance had not obliged. It had only buried the guilt more deeply.

"Dinner's ready," he called to Kelechi.

"That was quick." Kelechi sat down at the table, rubbing his stomach with anticipation.

Jebuni closed his eyes in prayer. "Father God, we thank You for this food. Bless it so it will nourish our bodies and sustain us. In the name of Jesus, I pray. Amen."

Kelechi picked up his sandwich. "Do you really think praying over your food makes a difference?"

"Absolutely. Praying always makes a difference, as long as one prays to the only true God."

Yet, why had praying not eased the pain of Jebuni's past? Why did the guilt still rage in his soul?

Why could he not forgive himself for Kofi's death?

He took a deep breath. He needed to stop blaming himself. This weather was negatively affecting him, bringing back unwelcome memories. He deliberately shook off his mood and began to eat.

"Where did you learn all of this stuff about prayer?" Kelechi bit into his sandwich.

"From American missionaries who came to Ghana. When I was just a lad, my mother started attending the church services of the missionaries and accepted Christ. She then started sending me to Sunday school where I, too, eventually accepted Jesus as my Savior and Lord."

Kelechi scratched his head. "To each his own. As for me, I am content to worship the gods of my ancestors—if I worship them at all." He laughed.

Jebuni's heart grieved for his friend. Kelechi had no idea of the personal loss—in both this life and the next—that awaited one who chose not to follow Christ. Jebuni would continue to pray for Kelechi, trusting that one day he, too, would see the light of truth.

After their meal together, Kelechi cleared the table while Jebuni washed and dried the dishes and put them back in the cupboard. If his tribe in Ghana could see him now, they would be shocked. No future heir to the chieftaincy ever lifted a finger to do housework. Housework was the domain of women, not men.

Especially not of royal men.

Jebuni put away the dishtowel and then made himself a cup of coffee to keep awake as he plunged into a long night of study. He would work extra tonight to make up for the time he would lose tomorrow evening to attend the art lecture. Perhaps there would be other Ghanaians present to comfort his heart. Perhaps, for a few hours, he would forget the guilt that gnawed at him, leaving him raw inside.

Perhaps one day he would be able to forgive himself for failing to rescue his friend from the jaws of death.

* * * *

Tori's heart surged with excitement as she and Anna entered the large, ornate, high-ceilinged room at the Philadelphia Museum of Art. Its mahogany-paneled walls provided a warm, inviting atmosphere for holding a lecture. Bronze wall sconces illuminated the room with a soft, yet bright, light. To the right of the entrance stood a mahogany table on which sat a large, engraved ceramic vase filled with white gardenias whose sweet fragrance floated through the air. All around her, the chattering of enthusiastic voices heralded an evening of good things to come. Already the room had filled almost to capacity with people eager to enjoy the rare lecture on Ghanaian art.

Since admission was free, seating was on a first-come, first-served basis. Tori scanned the room. Two seats in the center section sat empty.

She turned to Anna and then pointed. "Look! Two seats in the middle section, near the end of the row. Let's grab them."

Tori led the way, pushing gently through the crowded aisle full of people intently engaged in conversation. With purse in hand and Anna following close behind, she excused herself as she made her way through the row to the empty seats. She took the next-to-last spot, while Anna settled in the seat to Tori's left. A young black man occupied the last seat in the row, right next to the aisle.

Tori took off her coat and laid her purse on her lap.

"Hello." The man on her right greeted her with a brilliant smile and an unusual English accent.

Tori reciprocated the smile. "Hello." The man's deep-brown eyes were kind and his demeanor, dignified. She liked him instantly.

He extended his hand. "My name is Jebuni Kalitsi, but people call me Jeb. I am from Ghana."

"Really? Then you must be especially excited about this lecture."

"Quite excited, indeed."

To her great embarrassment, Tori suddenly realized she had not accepted his extended hand. "Oh, I'm so sorry." She shook his hand. It felt warm as it touched her skin. "My name is Victoria Pendola, but you can call me Tori. I'm happy to meet you, Jeb." She turned toward Anna. "This is my sister Anna."

Jeb leaned over and shook Anna's hand as well.

Tori turned toward him. "Are you visiting from Ghana?"

"Actually, I am a graduate exchange student at the University of Pennsylvania. I'm enrolled in the School of Economics."

"What a coincidence! I'm a grad student at Penn, too. I'm majoring in Art History with a concentration in African art."

Jeb's eyes widened. "Fascinating! Then you, too, must be excited about tonight's lecture."

"Very much so."

Jeb turned more fully toward her. "What is it you like about African art?"

Tori laughed. "Everything! I love its simplicity, its passion, its bright colors. I love its sense of youthfulness, balance, and proportion. One of my favorite artists is Amon Kotei."

Jeb nodded in approval, his gaze intent. "Kotei recently designed our Ghanaian coat of arms."

"Yes!" Tori smiled. "It's amazing!"

"You are right about the simplicity and passion of African art. In my homeland, we love the simple life with a passion. That love is expressed in our art."

A voice from the front of the room interrupted their conversation. "Good evening, ladies and gentlemen. We are about to begin, so would everyone please take his seat?"

Those few who remained standing quickly took their places as the speaker introduced the lecturer.

Trying hard to focus her attention, Tori listened to the expert art historian as he showed slides of the history of Ghanaian art. But the powerful presence of the man sitting beside her distracted her. Although they'd hardly spoken, she sensed there was something unique about him, something she'd never encountered in any other man. A quiet strength. A noble dignity.

A mysterious depth that begged to be explored.

She swallowed hard, half succeeding at reining in her roaming thoughts. As the evening progressed, every now and then she glanced over at Jeb. His eyes, more often than not, were on her rather than on the lecturer.

A pleasant shiver ran through her.

At the end of the lecture, the audience applauded with a standing ovation.

Tori turned toward Jeb and smiled at him. "That was wonderful, wasn't it?"

"Indeed." His medium-built, muscular frame exuded a gentle strength. Like velvet on steel. His intense gaze was upon her. "I have very much enjoyed meeting you, Tori."

"Likewise." Her heart caught in her throat.

"May I meet with you again some time to discuss Ghana and its art?"

Tori hesitated. She didn't even know this man. Yet, something inside her told her she could trust him. "Yes, I would enjoy meeting with you again to discuss Ghanaian art." She wanted to make clear that their meeting would be purely on the level of their shared interest in that topic. Secretly, however, her mind had already raced far ahead of that.

She reached into her purse for the little notebook and pencil she always carried and jotted down her phone number, and then tore out the page and handed it to Jeb with a smile. "The best time to reach me is in the late afternoon or early evening."

Jeb graciously took the note and gave her a little bow. "Very well, then. I will be in touch." He extended his hand again. "It was a pleasure to meet you, Tori." Then he reached over toward Anna. "It was a pleasure to meet you, Anna."

With that, he exited the row and left.

Anna nudged Tori in the elbow. "What was that all about?"

"I'm not quite sure. He asked if I would like to meet with him again to discuss Ghana and its art. I said I would."

"Are you sure he's interested only in discussing Ghana and its art?" Her sister's eyebrows arched.

"I'm not quite sure of that, either. The only thing of which I'm quite sure is that I felt something. An attraction between us."

"Yes, I noticed." Anna's voice was wry.

Tori looked at her sister. "Anna, were you eavesdropping?"

"Who, me? Eavesdropping? What do you mean?" Anna feigned innocence.

"Yes, you, my dear sister! You know exactly what I mean." Tori burst into laughter, her heart filled with a new joy she'd never experienced before. Something had happened to her tonight. She'd received something she had not expected. A gift. A gift of a friendship that somehow she knew, in the depths of her being, would have a profound impact on her life.

Tori turned to Anna. "So, what did you think of him?"

Anna hesitated. "He seemed very nice, but—"

"But what?"

"But you know how Pop hates colored people. He'll forbid you to befriend him."

Tori's muscles tensed. Anna was right. Pop had made his deeply ingrained prejudice against blacks audibly clear on several occasions throughout their lives. "Well, Pop doesn't have to know. At least, not just yet."

"Tori, you know as well as I do that if you end up dating this man, you can't keep it from Pop forever. Sooner or later you're going to have to tell him."

Tori's muscles tensed. "I guess I'll just make it later than sooner." She dismissed the alarming thought for now. "How about a cup of coffee before we go home?"

"That sounds like a good idea."

Arm in arm, the sisters walked toward a nearby café. As Tori breathed in the brisk night air, all she could think about was the intriguing man from Ghana named Jeb.

Chapter 2

Jeb gazed out the large window as the lumbering bus wended its way through city streets from the Philadelphia Art Museum to his dorm building. His mind could focus on nothing but the beautiful young American woman he'd met at the lecture. She'd magnetized him as no other woman ever had. Her enthusiastic demeanor, her childlike wonder, and her remarkable beauty had captured his attention.

He needed to see her again.

As the bus rolled down the brightly lit streets, stopping at each corner to pick up and discharge passengers, his thoughts drifted back to his homeland, his parents, and his people. His heart sank. Never would they permit his having a relationship with a white woman. Despite the move toward nationalism that had begun at the end of World War II, Ghana still held on to the vestiges of apartheid encouraged in Africa by the European colonialists over the past half century. Jeb bristled as he pictured the segregated bus stops, the public facilities, and the bicycle paths of his homeland where whites and blacks were forbidden to intermingle. So often, he'd watched in anger the despairing faces of blacks relegated to the back of the bus, while whites took seats at the front.

His heart ached at the many interracial love stories he'd heard of that never ended in marriage because of racism. So many dreams unfulfilled. So many hearts broken by a prejudice that brought only suffering and death.

He'd often wondered why blacks put up with such hateful treatment. Was it that they truly believed themselves to be inferior? Had generations of suppression etched a paradigm of inferiority in their thinking to the point that they now believed a lie? Had their souls been so diminished by the base treatment of the white man that they had no strength of will to fight back?

The injustice of it all gnawed at his insides.

But not only had he witnessed widespread prejudice in Ghana, he'd also seen it here in the States. People often crossed to the other side of the street when he approached. Although in America he was permitted to sit in the front of the bus, passengers boarding after him would, if possible, choose a seat far away from him. There seemed to be a widespread desire among whites to distance themselves from him. To avoid him.

To reject him.

Not everyone. But many.

He rubbed his chin and vowed to do whatever lay in his power to change things. If God gave him strength, he would eliminate the cancer of racial prejudice in Ghana, starting with his own tribe. He would help to make Ghana a country in line with the principles of freedom and equality that every human being deserved.

But what of Tori? He was definitely interested in getting to know her more. Could he risk placing her in emotional or physical jeopardy by asking her out on a date? Pursuing a relationship with her? As a white woman, she'd likely never experienced prejudice. What did she know of its searing rejection? Its blatant injustice? Its piercing pain? Was he willing to subject her to that pain?

Even more worrisome was her family. Would they permit her to pursue a relationship with a black man? And, although the idea was almost incomprehensible to consider after just meeting her, what would happen if the relationship progressed? What if one day he married her and brought her to Ghana? Would his family and tribe accept her?

Deep down, Jeb feared the answers to these troubling questions. Although his mother was a Christian, prejudice against whites was deeply ingrained in the Ghanaian people. Even the missionaries had fallen short of totally convincing them that the color of one's skin had nothing to do with the color of one's character. Old traditions had deep roots. Sometimes so deep that it took generations to disentangle and dislodge them.

Yet, before leaving to study abroad, Jeb had noticed the winds of change beginning to blow in his country. Ever so gently. A rising cry to end colonialism and apartheid had begun to sound throughout the land, igniting a fire in Jeb's heart. A fire that nothing could quench.

His mind returned to Tori. Why was he thinking of a long-term relationship with her anyway? Surely, he was jumping the gun. He'd just met her. He knew little about her except that she loved Ghanaian art. Why had he even asked to see her again? It would have been better to part ways and leave well enough alone.

Yet, his heart had taken the lead over his head. Something he was noted for doing. So often, his father had reprimanded him for not thinking things through first. Yet, every time Jeb had followed his heart instead of his head, he'd been right. Maybe it was what the American missionaries called being "led by the Spirit." As a young boy, Jeb had encountered Christ and had trusted His Holy Spirit ever since to lead him. Could he trust the Holy Spirit to guide him now?

Of course, he could.

And he would.

He whispered a prayer. "Father in heaven, You know my heart. It has been powerfully struck by the young woman Tori whom I met this evening. Even her name of Victoria—Victory—speaks to me. Father, I do not believe in coincidences. It was no coincidence she chose the seat next to me. I believe it was You who directed her to that seat. So, I ask, Father, that You would make Your will clear to me in this situation. I submit to Your will and only Your will. In Jesus' name I pray. Amen."

The bus stopped a block from Jeb's dorm building. Thanking the driver, Jeb stepped down into the cold November evening. A light rain fell on his bare head, chilling him to the bone. Not one accustomed to wearing hats, he wished he had one now.

He entered his building and took the stairs two steps at a time to his small apartment. He found Kelechi still awake, poring over his books.

Kelechi lifted his gaze from his studies. "Hey, man! How was the lecture?"

Jeb pulled up a chair and sat down at the table next to him. "You wouldn't believe what happened."

Kelechi leaned back in his chair and folded his hands over his chest. "You've met a girl and you've fallen in love—or at least in serious 'like'."

Jeb was taken aback. "How did you know?"

"The look on your face betrays you, man."

Jeb protested. "What look?"

Kelechi laughed. "The look of an utter idiot. A madman. I've seen that look before, and it spells nothing but trouble."

Jeb laughed. "She is the most intriguing woman I have ever met. She is beautiful, intelligent, kind and—

"And white?"

"Yes, white. How did you know that, too?"

"It's a question of the odds."

"So what if she is white?"

"Not a problem with me. But it could be a problem with others." Kelechi closed his book. "Jeb, you know we live in a society that treats blacks and whites differently. There's no denying it. Not only here in America, but especially in Africa."

Jeb released a long sigh. "You're right. Despite some laws to the contrary, what is on the books legally is not always what is in the heart morally."

Kelechi pointed at him. "And therein lies the problem."

"You're right again. The missionaries would often say that what is in the heart is what truly matters. The lips speak lies, but the heart never lies." Jeb rose and paced the room. He hated the racism that ascribed more intrinsic value to one group of people over another. Did not God create all men equal? Yet, that truth had been lost to those who hungered and thirsted for power. To those whose greed blinded them to universal truth. He stopped in front of Kelechi. "I don't see her as a white woman at all. I see her simply as a woman."

"That is a good start, my friend." Kelechi raised his arms and folded his hands at the nape of his neck. "So, tell me more about this woman of yours."

Jeb sat down again, blood rushing to his face. "Do you think interracial marriages will ever be fully accepted legally and socially?"

"Don't tell me you're thinking of marriage already! You just met the girl!"

"Yes, but deep down in my heart—I don't know why or how—I can't let go of the thought she might be the woman for me."

Kelechi grew serious. "Jeb, you're acting purely on emotion, and you know as well as I do emotions can be dangerous. They can change from one day to the next." Kelechi patted his friend on the shoulder. "I suggest you get a good night's rest and see how you feel in the morning. You may have an entirely different opinion of her tomorrow."

While Jeb knew Kelechi meant well, Jeb also knew Kelechi was wrong. A good night's sleep would not change his interest in Tori.

It would only strengthen it.

* * * *

Hunched over a stack of books, Tori sat in a cubicle at the university library. The bag lunch she'd brought with her still sat on the desk, untouched.

Nearly three long weeks had passed since the lecture, and she still had not heard from Jeb. Perhaps he'd changed his mind about calling her. Perhaps he hadn't meant what he'd said.

Perhaps he was afraid to call.

All kinds of negative thoughts bombarded her mind, robbing her of her peace. Yet, of the three possible reasons for his failure to call, the third one seemed the most viable. Tori's instinct told her Jeb was not the kind of person who would break his word.

She lassoed her mind and drew it back to the task at hand—her thesis paper on the Ghanaian artist Amon Kotei. The lecture on Ghanaian art had so inspired her that she'd chosen to do her final assignment on this well-known artist. The more she learned about him and his native land, the greater her desire to visit Ghana one day.

Truth be told, she also wanted to impress Jeb—should he ever call her. Since their meeting at the lecture, she'd thought of him constantly. His gentle ways. His radiant smile. His noble demeanor. There was something regal about him that defied description. She longed to get to know him better.

Taking in a deep breath, she did her best to push him out of her mind. Why should she set herself up for disappointment by continually dwelling on him? Yet, refusing to think about Jeb only made her think of him more.

Was she falling for him? This man she'd barely spoken to?

She glanced at her wristwatch. Four-thirty p.m. She'd been at the library all afternoon and had hardly accomplished anything. Time to pack up her things, check out her library books, and head home for dinner.

Upon arriving at the house, Tori found Anna and their mother bustling about in the kitchen as they prepared the evening meal.

Anna immediately stopped and smiled knowingly. "Jeb called."

Tori's heart leapt. "At what time?"

"About an hour ago. He said he would call back this evening at seven."

Mom cast a sidelong glance at Tori. "Who is Jeb?" Although her voice seemed matter-of-fact, Tori knew her mother well enough to know she was extending her protective antennae.

Tori tried to remain nonchalant. "Oh, he's just someone Anna and I met at the art lecture a few weeks ago."

"Why is he calling you?"

Tori's muscles stiffened. "He probably wants to discuss Ghanaian art."

Mom gave Tori a penetrating look but said no more.

A few minutes before seven, Tori positioned herself on the sofa next to the telephone. Her heart pounded. What would she say to Jeb when he called? It was one thing to talk with him among a crowd of people, but it was quite another to talk with him in a private telephone conversation. Well, semi-private. She wished Pop and Mom would leave the room. At least Anna, who'd gone to their bedroom, understood Tori's need to be alone. Wonderful, faithful Anna. Always sensitive to her sister's needs.

At 7:00 p.m. sharp, the telephone rang. Pop looked up and then returned to reading his newspaper. Mom glanced at Tori and then resumed her knitting. Neither of them left.

"Hello." Tori winced at the quiver in her voice.

"Tori? This is Jeb."

The sound of his baritone voice on the other end of the line was like the cascading of a waterfall. Rich, strong, and vibrant. Her heart stirred.

"Hello, Jeb. How nice to hear from you!" Was she coming across too happy? Too excited? Too eager?

"How are you doing?" She could hear the smile in his voice.

"Very well, thank you. And you?"

"Also well, thank you. I am following up on our initial encounter to ask if you would like to meet for coffee to continue our discussion of Ghanaian art."

Tori glanced at her parents. Pop's eyes were trained on her. Mom focused on her knitting, but it was clear she was all ears to the conversation.

"I would love to!"

Jeb laughed, that same contagious laugh that had rippled through her heart every time she'd thought about it the past few weeks. "Wonderful! There's a little place called the *Penn-Ultimate Café*, across from the Penn library, which would be a quiet place to chat. Shall we meet there tomorrow evening at seven?"

"I know exactly where it is. Yes. That would be fine."

"Okay, then. I look forward to seeing you again."

"Likewise." Tori hesitated. "Goodbye, Jeb."

"Until tomorrow evening … " His voice trailed off.

She was the first to hang up, her heart still pounding.

Pop folded his newspaper. "Who was that?"

"Oh, just a friend Anna and I met at an art lecture a few weeks ago." Tori worried that the quiver in her voice would betray her true emotions.

"When will I get to meet him?"

"I suppose at some point, if necessary."

Pop put down his newspaper. "'If necessary'?" His fatherly Italian protectiveness kicked in. "Tori, you know how I feel about wanting to meet any man who comes into your life."

"Yes, Pop. I know."

"Then when shall I meet this guy?"

She sighed. "Pop, I hardly know him. If I determine I want to get to know him better, I will introduce him to you." Truth be told, she'd already determined she wanted to get to know Jeb better, but she wasn't ready to introduce him to her father, especially given his hatred of Negroes.

"I'll hold you to that."

Tori did not reply.

For the moment, her father seemed satisfied.

Mom looked at her, her eyes a blend of understanding and concern.

Tori rose and excused herself, eager to rejoin Anna. She found her sister sitting on her twin bed in the room they'd shared since they were little girls.

Anna looked up.

"It was Jeb."

Anna laughed. "I knew that much. I'm the one who spoke with him earlier, remember? So, what did he want?"

"He wants to get together to continue our discussion on Ghanaian art."

"Sure." Anna chuckled, a hint of friendly jesting lacing her voice.

"I dread what will happen when Pop learns that Jeb is black."

"Take one thing at a time, Tori. You don't need to tell Pop just yet. Don't create problems where they don't exist."

"You're right." Tori released a long sigh. "Oh, Anna. Why am I so eager to see him again?"

"Because you're obviously falling for him."

"But I can't fall in love!"

"Why not?"

"Because I hardly know him, for one thing." Tori hesitated. "Because I'm not ready to, for another thing."

"Who's ever ready to fall in love?"

"This whole thing has taken me by surprise."

"Falling in love always does."

Tori smiled. "How do you know so much about falling in love?"

"I've been there."

Tori gasped. "Anna, you never told me you've been in love."

"There isn't much to tell. It never went anywhere."

How could Anna not tell Tori she'd had feelings for someone? Her sister's reticence astounded her. Perhaps there was more to Anna than Anna let on.

"Besides, I'm a good observer."

"Did you observe anything about Jeb?"

Anna nodded. "I observed he's quite smitten with you."

"Do you think so? We didn't have much time to speak with each other."

"I know so. He couldn't keep his eyes off you the whole lecture."

"Ah, so you weren't listening to the lecture." Tori laughed. "Now the truth comes out."

Anna chuckled. "What was going on to my right was far more interesting."

"Oh, Anna! I feel as though my whole world is turning upside down."

Anna smiled. "Or maybe it's turning right-side up."

* * * *

The next evening, Tori left right after dinner to meet Jeb, three weeks to the day of their first encounter. Her heart pounded as she got off the bus and walked the two blocks to the popular campus café where they'd arranged to meet.

The university campus around her buzzed with life. Students hustled to and fro, heading to various destinations. Bespectacled professors in heavy sweaters and patchwork scarves hurried by, carrying leather briefcases stuffed with papers. Deep in thought, they kept their eyes down, looking at their feet. Tori smiled as a group of chattering co-eds passed by her, laughing uproariously. Freshmen for sure.

The air smelled of snow to come. Above her, the whitish night sky, pregnant with gray-white clouds, seemed ready to give birth.

Tori pulled her coat collar more tightly around her neck to ward off the chill. Grateful she'd worn a hat, she shoved her gloved hands deep into the pockets of her black wool coat and tried to calm her racing heart. In a few moments, she'd be with Jeb again. Would their second meeting be as comfortable as their first? Would they have as much to talk about? Would they be drawn closer to each other?

Or farther apart?

She quickened her pace past storefronts that glittered with the decorative lights of Christmas. The big holiday was only a few weeks away. What if she could spend it with Jeb? Wouldn't that be wonderful?

But would her parents allow him into their home?

As she passed a gift shop, the sound of "O, Holy Night," playing from a loud speaker, floated through the air and stirred her heart. This same song had played in the background at the little church outside the city that memorable Christmas Eve, eight years earlier, when she'd become a Christian at the age of sixteen. Was God sending her a sign? Was He telling her that a relationship with Jeb was His will for her?

As she reached the *Penn-Ultimate Café*, Tori glanced through the large front window. Her heart skipped a beat. Jeb had already arrived and sat at a table toward the back of the tiny restaurant.

Taking a deep breath, she opened the front door and strode confidently inside, making her way toward the back past a few customers deep in conversation.

Jeb spotted her instantly and rose to greet her. "Tori, it is so good to see you again."

Her pulse quickening, she smiled. "Likewise, Jeb."

As she pulled off her gloves, he extended his hand to greet her.

Jeb helped her remove her coat and then pulled out a chair for her.

Her heart warmed at his chivalry.

When they were both seated, Jeb spoke first. "I want to thank you for accepting my invitation. I do not know American customs very well, so I informed myself as best I could as to how to invite a lady for coffee."

She smiled. His genuineness totally disarmed her. "I commend you. You gave a perfect invitation."

His big smile exuded great relief. "I was quite concerned I would say or do something inappropriate."

His humility melted her heart. "You don't ever have to worry about that with me."

Gratitude flickered in his eyes.

A waiter came to take their order. When he left, Jeb continued. "So, please tell me more about yourself. Were you born in Philadelphia?"

"No, but I was born nearby in a small town about thirty minutes from here called Valley Forge. Have you heard of it?"

"Yes, of course. It is one of the chief places where your famous Revolutionary War for independence from the British was fought under the command of General George Washington."

Tori smiled, impressed with his knowledge. "Exactly! I see you know American history."

"History is one of my favorite subjects. Since I was a boy, I have always been fascinated by it."

"I love history, too. That's one reason I'm enrolled in the art history program." She studied his face. The squareness of his jaw. The strength of his nose.

The smoothness of his lips ...

She cleared her throat. "Speaking of art history, what did you think of the lecture on Ghanaian art? From your perspective as a native of Ghana, was it accurate?"

"Most accurate, indeed. In fact, I was quite impressed with the speaker's depth of knowledge."

The waiter brought their coffees. Tori poured a teaspoon of sugar from the sugar dispenser and added it to her cup. "Ghana must be a lovely country."

A wistful look crossed Jeb's face. "For me, it is a lovely country. I cannot speak for others who do not know Ghana. Like all countries, we have our problems, but we also have our national pride."

Tori listened attentively as Jeb described his homeland. His eyes softened as he spoke, revealing not only his deep love for Ghana but also his homesickness for it.

"Will you be returning home soon?" She asked the question with trepidation.

"At the end of this academic year, when I finish my studies."

Tori forced herself to ignore the pang that news sent to her heart. "What will you do when you return?"

Jeb chuckled. "When I tell you what I'll be doing, will you promise not to get up and leave?"

His humorous comment surprised her. "Of course, I won't leave. That would be rude."

"Very well, then. I will tell you." He leaned forward and lowered his voice. "I do not make public the fact that I am the son of a tribal chieftain in the region of Ahanta and a successor to the chieftaincy. One day, I will become chief of my tribe and rule my people."

Tori's eyes grew wide. "So, I'm sitting in the presence of royalty?"

Jeb seemed a bit uncomfortable. "If you wish to look at it that way, yes."

She fumbled. "Well, what should I do now? Should I bow? Curtsy? Or move to another table?"

He laughed heartily, expressing his intense delight at her sense of humor.

"Nothing of the kind. Simply grace me with your presence." Intense feeling spread across his face as heat rose to hers.

Something clicked within her. Here she was, sitting in the presence of a king, and he desired *her* presence! What an amazing man!

Their eyes locked and, for a brief instant, all time stood still.

Tori swallowed hard. An ache rose from the depths of her heart. A longing to spend time with this man.

They spoke for several hours, never tiring. They discussed life, culture, and country. They explored art, politics, and apartheid. They spoke of their families and their beliefs, their hopes and their dreams, and were especially delighted—and relieved—to discover they were both Christians.

For Tori, where Jeb stood with God had been a question of the utmost concern. Since the Bible forbade marriages between believers and unbelievers, if Jeb had not been a Christian, she would not have been able to pursue a relationship with him. Learning that he was a believer removed that most important barrier.

At 10:45 p.m., the waiter announced that the café would close at eleven.

Tori glanced at her watch. "Oh, my! I had no idea it was so late. I've probably kept you from your studies. I'm so sorry!"

"Not at all. I had planned to devote the entire evening to you."

A pleasant chill coursed through her veins.

They rose and Jeb helped Tori with her coat.

As they left, Tori couldn't help but notice the disapproving stares on the faces of some of the customers, but she brushed them aside.

Jeb insisted on accompanying her to the bus stop and making sure she got safely on the bus.

As they waited, their breath formed puffs of clouds in the cold night air.

Jeb turned toward her, his eyes clear and bright. "When may I see you again?"

She wanted desperately to say she wished to see him every single moment she could, possibly even for the rest of her life. "I'm in class from Monday to Friday, but free most days in the late afternoons and early evenings. A couple of times a week, I work as a hostess at a restaurant in Center City, but my schedule varies from week to week. I'm also free on Saturday and Sunday afternoons."

"I will call you soon. Do you like classical music?"

"I love it, especially Baroque music."

He smiled broadly. "Ah! Another thing we have in common. I will arrange dinner in the city followed by a Baroque concert at the Academy of Music."

"I would enjoy that very much."

He took her hand and shook it gently, holding it just a bit longer than necessary. "Thank you, Tori, for the most wonderful evening of my life."

Surprised by his words, her gaze lingered on his ever so briefly, but just long enough to read something in his eyes that both excited her and frightened her.

Was Jebuni Kalitsi falling in love with her?

Chapter 3

The sound of the ringing telephone startled Jeb out of a deep sleep, a sleep hard come by after the last three exciting weeks of dating Tori.

He turned on his bedside lamp and glanced at his clock. Three thirteen a.m. Who could be calling at this hour? And why?

His muscles tensed.

He shifted onto his elbow to pick up the receiver. "Hello."

"Hello. This is the international operator. I have a call from Ghana for Jebuni Kalitsi." A barely audible woman's voice spoke on the other end of the line. Jeb's pulse quickened. "This is he." He threw his legs over the side of the bed and sat up straight.

"Please stay on the line. I will connect you momentarily."

Only a tragedy could prompt a call from Ghana. Making such a telephone call required a two-hour trip from his village to a central location that provided a telephone. To make the trip usually implied the urgent need to transmit bad news. Otherwise, one would simply send a letter or a telegram.

Jeb tried to quiet his racing mind and rapidly beating heart.

After a series of brief exchanges among several operators between the United States and Ghana, he was finally connected.

"Jebuni. This is Adofo." His brother's voice on the other end of the line was strained and slightly garbled, making it difficult for Jeb to hear him clearly.

Jeb pressed the receiver more closely against his ear. "What is it, my brother? Is everyone all right?"

"Jebuni, Papa has died."

A bombshell struck the pit of Jeb's stomach, robbing him of breath. For a moment, he could not speak. "Tell me what happened." He rubbed his hand over his stinging eyes.

"When Papa retired for bed last night, he complained of not feeling well. This morning, when Mama returned from the village market, he was not waiting for her on the veranda as usual. When she searched for him, she found him dead in bed."

Jeb's stomach clenched. "I will catch the first plane out of Philadelphia. Don't worry. I will be home soon. Is anyone with Mama?"

"I have been with her, of course, as well as many from the village, including the tribal elders. They will help us take care of matters until you arrive."

"I will be there as quickly as I can."

"Very well." His brother's voice seemed void of emotion. Perhaps he was in a state of shock. The younger of the two brothers born to their mother and father, Adofo's name meant *warrior*. His brusque manner matched. Over the years, the two brothers had not gotten along particularly well. Adofo seemed to envy Jeb his intelligence, his wit, and his favored position as the firstborn son. But Adofo compensated for his inferior feelings in physical strength and prowess. He was, however, gullible and a bit naïve about life.

"I should arrive tomorrow night your time. Meanwhile, I will pray."

Ignoring the comment, Adofo bid him goodbye and ended the call.

Dazed, Jeb replaced the receiver. His gut wrenched with the agony of losing the man he loved and adored more than any other man on earth. His mind whirled at a thousand miles an hour, trying to sort out the full meaning of the tragic news. To comprehend its implications on his life.

And on Tori's.

Now that his father was dead, the chieftaincy would fall to him as the firstborn son. What would that mean to his relationship with Tori? The feelings he had for her had grown, and he believed Tori felt the same way about him. He'd fostered hope for what that meant for their future together. He'd even allowed himself to think he'd found a wife in her. If only he'd had time to get the tribal elders to reconsider their age-old tradition of choosing the chief's wife. But now that his father had died suddenly and Jeb was the new chief, there was no time. The new chief would need a wife, and the tribe would choose that wife for him. The tribe would not approve of a marriage to a woman they had not chosen for him.

Especially a white woman.

The thought unnerved him, but sufficient for the day were the evils thereof. He had enough to handle now with the sudden death of his father.

Jeb got out of bed and called the Philadelphia airport. "When is the next flight to Accra?"

"The next flight leaves Philadelphia at 2:07 p.m. this afternoon with a two-hour layover in New York. May I book your reservation, sir?"

"Yes, please do."

Jeb gave all the required information and hung up. He next arranged for a rental car to take him from Accra to his hometown of Sekondi, 225 kilometers from the airport and a four-hour trip by car. Adding that to the sixteen-hour flight, he estimated he would be arriving at his mother's house around dinnertime the next evening. Finally, he called the taxicab company to request a cab to pick him up at noon to take him to the airport.

With travel arrangements taken care of, Jeb grabbed his suitcase from the closet and packed enough for a two-week stay, not knowing for sure what he would find when he got home.

He had much to do before he left the States. He would need to notify his professors and arrange for missed classes. To his relief, his exams were not scheduled until mid-January, after the Christmas break.

As the truth of his father's death struck him with full force, an anguished sob rose from the depths of Jeb's chest. Overwhelmed with grief, he threw himself on his bed and wept uncontrollably. Memories of his father flooded his mind. Memories of shared hunting trips deep into the wilds. Of fishing trips on the Pra River in Shama.

Of late night talks about God and life.

Jeb swallowed hard. He hadn't seen his father in two years—since he'd left to study in the United States—and now he regretted the long absence despite the frequent letters they'd exchanged. Often, over the years he'd been home, his father had spoken of Jeb's succession to the chieftaincy, grooming him for the role of future leader of the tribe. Now, sooner than they'd expected, the chieftaincy would fall to him.

"It is a sacred trust, Jebuni." Papa would square his jaw as his eyes narrowed with the seriousness of the matter. "A trust you must carefully and faithfully uphold in order to protect the people and to continue the legacy of the Kalitsi name with honor."

Then Papa would lean forward on his royal stool, hand-made of *sese* wood, and a symbol of his identity and governance, and fold his hands on his lap. Looking deep into Jeb's eyes, he would say, "My son, do not fail those who have gone before you, but continue their legacy of truth, honor, and peace. Upon my death, you will raise up my fallen stool and take your proper place. I am counting on you, and so is our tribe."

And now that day had come. Like a bolt of lightning. Sudden. Unexpected.

Terrifying.

The tribal stool had fallen, and it was time for Jeb to raise it up again.

His body shook as hot tears drenched his pillow. By the time he'd spent his tears, the fingers of dawn had parted the morning sky, revealing a canvas of purple-gray and rose.

His thoughts turned to Tori. He would have to notify her of his departure. They had planned several dates over the Christmas break. *The Nutcracker* at the Academy of Music. The Christmas lights at Wanamaker's, followed by lunch in the Crystal Room. A walk through the Christmas Village at Strawbridge's.

Sadly, he would have to postpone them until his return.

A sudden thought struck him. What if he could not return? What if his tribe insisted that he remain to rule them and that they choose his wife for him?

What if he insisted that he would accept the chieftaincy only if he could choose his own wife?

While a tribe could not force a man to be chief, refusing the chieftaincy was greatly frowned upon. Caught between the woman he loved and his royal duty, Jeb would be hard-pressed to reconcile the two without forfeiting the throne. Yet, to forfeit the throne would be to betray his father.

Jeb glanced at the clock. Six-twenty-three a.m. Soon Kelechi would awaken.

Jeb took a quick shower and dressed. His packing finished, he brewed himself a cup of coffee and awaited Kelechi in the kitchen.

In a few moments, his roommate entered. "What are you doing up? And dressed already?"

"I have some bad news. I got a call from Ghana. My father has died."

Startled into wakefulness, Kelechi placed a hand on Jeb's shoulder. "I am so sorry, my friend!"

"My brother called shortly after three this morning."

"Why didn't you wake me?"

"It was not necessary. I did not want to disturb your sleep. I took the time to make my plane reservations, to shower and dress, and to pack. My flight doesn't leave until this afternoon. It is the earliest one I could get from Philadelphia."

Kelechi settled into a chair next to Jeb. "What can I do to help you?"

"Perhaps you could contact my professors to tell them that my father died and that I had to leave right away."

"Yes, I would be happy to do that for you. How long will you be gone?"

"I have no idea. I am guessing that it will be for at least two weeks, if not longer. I will need to help my brother with the legal matters surrounding my father's death." He hesitated. "And now that my father is gone, I will be expected to assume the leadership of the tribe."

Kelechi raised an eyebrow. "What does that mean for your studies?"

"It is unclear. The tribal elders might be willing to allow me to return to finish my studies before becoming chief—or they might not."

"I see there is much to think about, isn't there? I wish you wisdom and peace."

"Thank you. I will need both."

"What about Tori?"

Jeb had told Kelechi of his strong feelings for Tori. Those feelings had only intensified since meeting her. He'd never felt this way about a woman. Not that he'd had any deep relationship over the course of his life. Yet, Tori had struck a profound chord in his heart, a chord that would not stop vibrating. Jeb looked intently at Kelechi. "Would you keep an eye on her for me?"

"Of course."

"I plan to call her at seven and hope to see her before I leave."

Kelechi nodded. "She will be deeply grieved at your loss."

She would, indeed. Over the weeks, she'd asked Jeb so many questions about his family—his father, his mother, his brother. Every time Jeb had spoken about his father, Tori had remarked on the beauty of their relationship. She'd also recounted the hardships of her relationship with her own father. She'd expressed a desire one day to meet Jeb's father, a desire that had deeply pleased him.

Now that desire would never be fulfilled.

And now that he would soon assume the chieftaincy, what would become of their relationship?

A new rush of grief swept over Jeb.

"Is there anything more I can do to help?" Kelechi's voice interrupted Jeb's thoughts.

"No, thank you. Not at the moment." Jeb reached out toward Kelechi to embrace him. "I will miss you, my friend."

"I will miss you, too."

"I don't know when I will return."

Kelechi put a hand on Jeb's shoulder. "I will hold down the fort while you're gone."

"Be sure not to burn it down with your cooking." Jeb made a feeble attempt at humor.

"I wouldn't dare. I'd have *you* to face when you get back." Kelechi smiled through misty eyes. "Well, I have to leave for my first class. I wish you well, Jebuni, and look forward to your return."

Jeb nodded, a lump forming in his throat.

"And don't worry about Tori." He pointed to himself. "Old Kelechi here will take good care of her."

Jeb managed a smile. "I have no doubt that you will."

Kelechi grabbed his books from the table and left.

* * * *

As Tori applied the finishing touches on her makeup before leaving for classes, the telephone rang. Who would be calling this early in the morning?

Her sister joined her in front of the bathroom sink. "It's Jeb," she whispered. "Thankfully, I answered the telephone instead of Pop or Mom."

Thankfully, indeed! Because of her father's prejudice against blacks, Tori had been forced to keep her relationship with Jeb hidden from him. It was not something she wanted to do, but Pop would never approve of her dating a black man. As for her mother, Mom went along with her husband in order to avoid a family feud. Anna was Tori's only confidante.

Tori gasped. "What's wrong?"

"I don't know. I didn't ask. But he sounded quite upset."

Tori dropped everything and hurried to the living room. Grateful that her parents were not in the room, she picked up the receiver. "Jeb?"

"Tori, I have some bad news."

Her muscles tensed.

"I received word this morning from home that my father has died. I must leave immediately."

Tori's heart sank. "Oh, Jeb! I am so sorry! When will you be leaving?"

"My flight departs this afternoon at two o'clock. It was the earliest flight I could get."

"How long will you be gone?"

"I cannot say for sure, but it's likely I will have to remain for at least two weeks. There will be many legal matters to handle, especially since I am the firstborn son."

Tori's mind spun. Jeb had often mentioned that, upon his father's death, he would be required to assume the leadership of the tribe. But that day had seemed so far away that she had deemed it almost impossible. Now it was upon her, and the reality of the situation struck her with full force. Dare she ask him the question burning in her heart?

"I suppose you will now be required to assume the chieftaincy?" Her heart pounded as she waited for his reply, knowing already what it would be.

He hesitated. "That is one of the matters I will be handling while I am home."

She would not press him further. "I will be praying for you."

"Thank you, Tori. I would like to see you before I leave."

"And I, you." Her voice quivered.

"Perhaps you can see me off at the airport?"

"I would love to. I'll be there at one o'clock."

At 1:00 p.m., Tori arrived at the Philadelphia International Airport. She quickly paid the driver and exited the cab that had dropped her off at the curb in front of the domestic flight terminal. Since there were no direct flights to Ghana from Philly, Jeb would have to fly to New York's Idlewild Airport, where the flight would stop on its way to Ghana.

The late December day was cold and blustery, sending a chill through Tori's bones. As she hurried toward the large glass door to the terminal, a light wind rustled a few remaining fallen leaves across the sidewalk, while icy raindrops prickled her face.

She welcomed the warm rush of heat as she entered the terminal. People hustled to and fro, heading to various destinations to celebrate the Christmas holidays. All around her, multicolored lights twinkled on storefronts in anticipation of the season. Melodious strands of Christmas carols filled the air as she hurried toward the gate where Jeb awaited her.

Despite the joyful atmosphere, Tori's heart was heavy. Heavy because she'd planned to celebrate Christmas with Jeb. But now Christmas wouldn't be the same.

Tori took the escalator to the second floor two steps at a time and hurried down the corridor, past swarms of passengers traveling to and from all parts of the world. The sound of chatter filled the air, while the aroma of freshly brewed coffee and hot cinnamon buns wafted to her nostrils from a nearby coffee shop. In the distance, the sound of airplanes taking off and landing echoed in her ears.

She quickened her step, hoping to spend as much time as possible with Jeb before his departure.

Her heart pounded as she drew closer to the gate where he waited for her.

She found him standing in front of the huge window that overlooked the tarmac. Her heart melted at the sight of his broad shoulders and solid physique. Outside, a large plane was being prepared for departure.

Smiling, Tori tapped Jeb on the shoulder from behind.

Jeb swung around and immediately took her into his arms. "Oh, Tori! I am so grateful you have come. I needed to see you."

His breath was warm against her cheek.

Her heart soared at his overwhelming reception. Being in his arms—even for an instant—was like heaven on earth. She never wanted it to end.

Jeb led her to the first row of seats facing the window and sat down at her side, turning toward her. "I cannot thank you enough for coming."

"I wouldn't have had it any other way."

"I was afraid I would not get to see you before I left."

She studied his eyes, red-rimmed from weeping. "I am so sorry to hear about your father."

"Thank you. He was a great man."

She smiled. "I have no doubt. All I have to do is look at you to know that."

He took her hands, his look intense. "Tori, there is much I must tell you before I leave. And not much time to tell it."

Her heart tensed as she listened.

"The death of my father is not an ordinary occurrence in my culture. As you know, my father was the chief of our tribe. Now that he has died, I, as his firstborn son, must assume succession to the throne—or, as we call it in Ghana, the stool."

"What does that mean?"

"It means that I will have to return to Ghana permanently and make my life there."

Her muscles tightened. "Does that mean you won't be coming back?"

"I don't know for sure. I am going to request permission from the tribal elders to complete my studies. If they agree, I will return to finish my degree." He paused. "But then I would have to return to Ghana after graduation in May to assume my position as chief."

Tears welled up in Tori's eyes. "I see." She swallowed hard and lowered her gaze. Her life—the dream she'd barely begun to hope for during their whirlwind romance—was falling apart right before her very eyes. She sighed and then raised her gaze toward him again. "I guess that means our lives will go in different directions."

Without responding to her question, his gaze locked on to hers. "There is one more thing."

Tori's stomach clenched. What could be worse than never seeing Jeb again?

"It is the custom of my tribe to choose the chief's wife from among the tribal women."

Tori froze. Her heart lodged in her throat. The weight of Jeb's words pressed hard on her chest, choking the very breath out of her.

Her thoughts raced. Had Jeb not known about this custom all along? Why, then, had he led her on with their relationship? Why had he not told her before now?

Before she'd fallen madly in love with him?

Her blood temperature rose. "Why did you wait until now to tell me the elders must choose your wife from the women of the tribe?" Tori didn't want to add to Jeb's already great grief upon losing his father, but she had to know. Even if her question implied that she'd hoped their relationship would lead to his choosing her as his wife.

Sorrow and guilt etched Jeb's face. "Because I didn't think it would ever happen. I didn't think my father would die before I married. I thought I would be able to choose my own wife before becoming chief."

Tori's heart plummeted to her feet. "So, now that it has happened—now that you *are* chief—you must comply with the custom." The words slipped out of her mouth in a somber statement of fact.

Jeb nodded.

"But you're the chief! Can't you do what you want?"

"I know it is difficult for you to understand, but in my country, the tribe has much sway over the chief."

Jeb was right. It was very difficult for her to understand. She'd grown up in a country where individual freedom was the norm. How horrible not to be able to choose one's spouse!

She searched Jeb's eyes and read the turmoil there. Clearly, he was torn between his feelings for her and the chieftaincy. Would he be forced to make a choice between the two? If so, which would he choose? Her or the chiefdom?

Tori's heart sank. If ever she wanted to die, it was now. In a single moment, all of her dreams of the past several weeks had been brutally dashed. Now that Jeb was the new tribal chief, there seemed to be little hope for their relationship.

Jeb reached for her hands, but she drew back. Was he playing tricks with her heart? Had he led her this far only to drop her like the proverbial hot potato?

Only to shatter her heart, leaving her alone to pick up the pieces?

No. She wouldn't take the bait. Despite her breaking heart, she would maintain her dignity. After all the years of enduring her father's indifference, she would not endure yet another rejection.

Especially when this time it came from the man she loved.

"Tori, what's wrong?"

"What's wrong? How can you ask such a question? Can't you see? What's wrong is that you and I are finished. You must go your way and I—." She choked back a sob. "I must go mine."

He remained silent, confirming the fear that had begun to gnaw at her soul. The truth was Jeb didn't love her. As calm as he was acting, there was no way he could. All these weeks, she'd misinterpreted his kindness. His enthusiasm. His interest.

Maybe the truth was he'd only wanted someone with whom to discuss Ghanaian art—as he'd said when he'd first met her. Maybe the truth was he was lonely and needed someone to share his favorite activities with him.

Maybe the truth was that, to Jeb—as well as to her father—she was little more than an accident of life. A temporary passerby.

One Jeb could put aside when he tired of her.

She took a deep breath and rose to leave. No use continuing a relationship that was going nowhere.

A relationship that she now saw had been doomed from the start.

"I'm glad I got to see you before you left. Please give my condolences to your family."

Jeb rose, too, his gaze interlocking with hers. "As soon as the tribe determines whether or not I can return to my studies, I will let you know."

She nodded. "I hope you will be able to." She looked at him, tears spilling onto her cheeks. "For your sake, and for your tribe's."

His jaw quivered as he took her hands. "I hope to see you again soon, Tori."

"If the Lord wills." Despite her sorrow, she wanted to hold him forever and never let him go.

"Yes, if the Lord wills."

A voice over the loudspeaker called for Jeb's flight to board. He picked up his carry-on bag. "It's time for me to go." His gaze rested upon her. "Take care of yourself while I'm gone."

She smiled through her tears. "You take care of yourself, too."

"If all goes well, I'll be back in a matter of weeks."

"Yes, if all goes well." Her voice drifted off.

"Goodbye, Tori."

"Goodbye, Jeb."

He walked toward the exit to board the plane. Once there, he turned and waved to her one last time.

Tori waved back. When he disappeared, she let loose on the shores of her cheeks the tidal wave of hot tears that had been crashing against the back of her eyes.

* * * *

Jeb wanted to kick himself. Kick himself as he'd never kicked himself before. How could he have been so stupid? So afraid?

So cowardly?

He'd wanted so much to tell Tori he loved her. He'd wanted so much to take her into his arms and never let her go.

He'd wanted so much to ask her to marry him.

But he'd been afraid. Afraid of making a choice his people would refuse. Afraid of leading her into a lifestyle so different from her own that he worried she'd never be happy.

He'd been a coward.

Just as he'd been when Kofi drowned at sea.

A chill ran through Jeb. He shook his head to dismiss the tormenting memory.

Would he forever be a weakling?

Engines roaring, the plane to Accra via New York lifted off the ground into the vast, pale-blue sky of the late-December day. The clatter of dishes in the galley kitchen mingled with the enthusiastic chatter of passengers in a cacophonous concert of sound.

As Jeb looked out the window, the buildings below stood like hundreds of pieces on a child's game board. Soon, they receded into the distance.

Would Tori recede as well?

His heart clenched. Never! She was too much a part of his present. And more than anything, he longed for her to be a part of his future as well.

But even setting aside the obstacle of choosing the woman he loved for his bride, he and Tori came from totally different worlds. For him, a life in Ghana would be what he'd always known. For Tori, it would mean a radical change toward a lesser life. One fraught with prejudice, rejection, and pain. A life of hardship that could turn her love for him—he dared to believe she loved him—into hatred.

Had he been willing to risk that? To risk her well-being for his selfishness? How could he do that to her if he truly loved her?

For the first time since beginning their courtship, he honestly acknowledged the obstacles to a future with her. Self-doubts cascaded over him as guilt pierced his soul. He'd been selfish. He'd thought only of his own desires and needs. Why hadn't he thought of her and of what a relationship with him would mean for *her* life? For *her* future? What had ever made him think he was worthy of her? What had prompted him to pursue a relationship with her?

What had made him fall head-over-heels in love with her?

He tensed. He'd been living in the bubble of a fantasy world. A bubble that had sheltered and protected their love from reality.

A bubble that would never burst.

Or so he'd thought.

But now, with the death of his father, the fantasy had died, leaving Jeb with the most difficult choice of his life: marry Tori or take his rightful position as tribal chief.

Would he assume his father's legacy? Or would he marry the woman he loved and give up the chieftaincy and the life he knew?

Either choice would mean a personal death for him. Yet, he couldn't have it both ways. Not while apartheid still reigned supreme in Africa. Not while the tribal elders vehemently opposed his marrying outside his tribe.

Not while his family forbade his marriage to a white woman.

He'd been a fool to try and pretend that that specter hadn't loomed over every moment of his time with Tori.

He drew in a deep breath. What should he do? His heart told him one thing, while his head told him another.

Weary with it all, Jeb closed his eyes in prayer. Only God knew the future. Only God had the answer to his dilemma.

Only God could reconcile the conflict in his heart.

But the big question remained: Was he willing to do whatever God told him to do? Or would cowardice yet again prevail in his life?

Jeb tried to swallow the painful lump that lodged in his throat. If only Tori knew who he really was. Not the strong, brave chief she believed him to be, but a weak, gutless man who did not even have the courage to proclaim his feelings for the woman he loved. A man who'd betrayed his best friend by failing to save his life.

A man unworthy of her.

He blinked back the stinging tears. No, he wasn't worthy of Tori Pendola. Better that she find a man who was her equal in virtue and valor. Someone who could give her the good life to which she was accustomed. A white man whose presence in her life would not arouse public disdain and alienation.

Better that he marry the woman the tribe chose for him and forget Tori.

He rubbed his eyes. Maybe he could rub away the indelible impression Tori had made on his heart.

But everywhere he looked, her face was before him, beckoning him with her deep hazel eyes in which he longed to swim. Her laugh, in which he longed to immerse himself.

Her heart, with which he longed to entwine his.

"Would you like a cold drink?" The cheerful voice of the stewardess interrupted Jeb's thoughts.

He nodded. "Seltzer water, please."

The attendant smiled and handed him a bottle of the carbonated beverage.

"Thank you."

"You're welcome, sir. Have a pleasant flight."

A pleasant flight. How could anything be pleasant without Tori?

Jeb leaned his head against the headrest. By now, the plane had reached cruising altitude. In less than an hour, it would land at Idlewild Airport where he would have a two-hour layover before his flight departed for Ghana.

As he stared out the window across the endless blanket of white cumulus clouds that lay like a field of cotton beneath him, he searched his heart for the answer to his prayer.

But all he heard was silence.

Chapter 4

Tori could not flee the airport fast enough. Heaving with sobs, she ran out of the terminal and climbed into the first taxicab parked alongside the curb in front of the terminal. The driver was an elderly gentleman about sixty years of age, with white hair and a matching beard trimmed close to his chin. He reminded Tori of her grandfather.

He smiled when she first entered, but then the look on his face became troubled.

After composing herself long enough to give the driver her destination, Tori retrieved her handkerchief from her purse and continued to weep softly.

"Are you all right, miss?" Genuine concern laced the cabbie's Irish brogue.

"No." She sniffled. "Truth be told, I'm miserable."

"Sorry to hear, miss." He glanced over his shoulder to the back seat where Tori sat. "Do you need a listenin' ear?"

She took a deep breath. "I need more than that. I need a new life."

He pulled away from the curb, around a parked bus, and into the traffic headed out of the airport. "Sounds to me like me very own words when I was your age." He glanced at her through the rearview mirror. "Words I spoke when I lost the girl I loved."

Tori's ears pricked. "How did you know?"

"Know what?"

"That I just lost the man I love."

"Just a good guess on my part. No woman cries like that unless she's lost someone she loves deeply. Usually a man."

In a few moments, they exited the airport and were on the main road leading to Center City.

Her curiosity aroused, Tori questioned the cabbie. "So, what did you do?"

"I did what every able-bodied man would do who'd lost the love of his life. I cried me heart out." He smiled gently. "Just like you."

There was something about his compassion that touched Tori's heart. "I promise not to drench your upholstery."

"No need to be worryin' yourself about that. The upholstery can take a beatin' better than the heart."

Dare she ask this total stranger the question that was on her mind? "Did you ever get back together again?" She paused. "With the girl, I mean?"

"Can't say that I did." His voice was wistful.

Tori's heart lurched. What if she never got back together with Jeb? What if she never saw him again?

What if she'd just said goodbye to him for the last time?

"How did you go on?"

"For a while, I doubted I could. In fact, methought I'd die for sure." He smiled and looked at her through the rearview mirror. "But I learned a good lesson through that whole ordeal."

"What?"

"I learned that the good Lord always knows what He's doin'. We just have to trust Him."

The cabbie's words brought her under conviction. God had never failed her in the past. Why would he fail her now? Tori swallowed hard. But how could she trust God in the midst of such heartache? Had He brought Jeb into her life only to snatch him away forever? Had He watched her fall in love with Jeb only to destroy that love?

Why would God do that?

"Did you ever learn what happened to your girl?"

The driver nodded. "She married someone else. Someone better suited to her."

Tori tensed. "And you?" Was she being too bold in asking?

"As for me, God gave me the best wife a man could ever ask for. Had I not met me Molly, I would've never learned the true meaning of love."

Well, that may have been fine for the cab driver. But it wasn't fine for Tori. She didn't want Jeb to marry anyone else. She wanted him to marry her. Nor did she want to marry anyone else. Only Jeb.

The cabbie cleared his throat. "Here's givin' you a piece of advice as if you was me own daughter."

But Tori didn't want any advice. She wanted Jeb.

"God's plan for your life is always better than your own." The cabbie's voice echoed in her ears, like the sound coming from a deep cavern. Garbled and difficult to understand.

Was it that she didn't want to understand? That her pain was too deep? What was there to understand anyway? That God had taken from her the man who had become so precious to her? That her dreams had just been shattered?

The cabbie's pious platitudes about God's plans for her life rang hollow in Tori's heart. What about *her* plans for her life? Wasn't she allowed to have her own plans? Did her life always have to depend on someone else's plans? Plans that sometimes backfired? Like her parents' plans that had backfired, resulting in her birth?

She was tired of being an accident in someone else's life. Tired of being rejected because of messing up the plans of others.

Tired of not being wanted.

If she made her own plans for her life, she could stop being an accident. She could order her life according to her will.

And then she'd be accepted for who she was.

That's what she'd found in Jeb. A man who accepted her for who she was. No strings attached. A man who did not consider her an accident, who was glad she was alive.

Or so she'd thought until today.

A sob escaped her throat. Apparently, she'd been wrong about Jeb all along. If he truly loved her, he wouldn't be in such conflict, would he? He'd know what to do without any doubt whatsoever.

The cabbie approached Tori's house. "I pray, lassie, that one day you'll come to understand that God's ways are better than our ways."

A tear trickled down her cheek. Deep down, she knew he was speaking truth. But embracing that truth was something her heart was not ready to do.

As they approached Tori's house, she calculated the time. Soon Jeb would arrive in New York and then depart for Ghana.

Tori paid the cab driver and thanked him for his kindness.

"One day, lassie, you'll make some man a fine wife. Mark me words."

But the only words Tori wanted to mark were the words "I do" that she'd hoped Jeb would one day speak to her in front of a church altar.

* * * *

A gray sky draped Ghana's Cape Coast Drive as Jeb covered the miles homeward toward Sekondi-Takoradi. The trip from the States to Ghana had been long and wearisome. Now that he was on the last leg of his journey, he longed to lay down his head for a good night of rest.

But there would be no rest. The most challenging part of his journey still lay ahead of him. His father's funeral. His appearance before the tribal council to determine his qualifications for assuming the chieftaincy.

His long and lonely separation from Tori.

Leaving her at the airport had rent his heart in two. Worst of all, he'd left her wondering about his feelings for her. He wouldn't be surprised if she never wanted to see him again.

Pushing aside the distressing thought, he scanned the roadside as he drove. Ghana had not changed much in the two years he'd been away. Apartheid still held sway, as he'd noticed upon his arrival in Accra. Public facilities were still segregated, and blacks and whites still lived their lives separated by the ridiculous and tenuous boundary of skin color.

Would the prejudice ever end?

Jeb's heart sank as he passed the area of the Cape Coast Castle, the deplorable prison where slaves were kept centuries before to await deportation to America. Slavery had been a blight to Ghana, and to every other country in which it had been practiced. Although physical slavery was no longer legal in his native land, prejudice continued overtly as a vicious and deceptive form of mental slavery. He'd experienced it both in Ghana and in the United States. And he'd hated it in both places.

But fighting the forces of apartheid in Africa would be no small task. Jeb would focus his burning passion for freedom on the small portion of earth God had given him to rule: his tribe. He would do everything in his power to abolish slavery in whatever form it reared its ugly head—physical, mental, spiritual, or financial—wherever he encountered it. Slavery diminished man and reduced him to only a specter of what he was created to be. Even animals treated one another better than man treated his fellow man.

As the new chief of his tribe, he would work hard to abolish prejudice in all of its forms.

If, of course, the tribe still wanted him as its chief.

When they discovered he did not want to marry a woman from his tribe, what would they do? Worse yet, when they discovered he wanted to marry a white woman, would they dismiss him altogether?

But worst of all, if they thought he was a coward, would they deny him the chieftaincy? So far, he'd been able to hide what he thought about himself. He'd put on a good front of bravery. Competence.

Strength.

But when the truth emerged—as it had at the airport with Tori— Jeb feared he would be fully exposed for who he truly was.

Nothing but a wimp.

He swallowed hard, straining to keep his eyes on the boring two-lane road that stretched ahead, long and narrow. Every now and then, he passed a cluster of thatched-roof hamlets surrounded by children at play in the twilight and old men sitting under straw hats while the women crafted shawls and scarves from multi-colored *kente* cloth.

Yes, this was the Ghana he remembered. This was the Ghana he missed.

This was the Ghana to which he hoped to return and spend the rest of his life.

But would Ghana still have a place for him?

The nearly twenty-four-hour trip from Philadelphia had left him exhausted, both physically and emotionally. He'd hardly slept during the flight, and the four-hour drive from Accra to Sekondi-Takoradi was monotonous, except for the sporadic, beautiful views of the coastline— views marred only by the worst memory of his life.

Jeb's mind drifted back to that horrific day. He was sixteen. The day was hot. He'd invited Kofi to go fishing offshore at Busua Beach, a tiny fishing village about forty-two kilometers west of their hometown. Kofi had been reluctant to go but had finally agreed.

The boys stood on the shore with their little fishing boat.

"Jeb, those look like storm clouds in the distance." Kofi's voice was tense.

Jeb shrugged off the warning. "Don't worry. They're far enough away not to cause a problem. By the time they get here, we'll be home having supper." He laughed.

Kofi hesitated. "I'm not so sure. Maybe we should forget the fishing trip for today."

"What? Are you scared?" Jeb teased.

Kofi gave him a questioning look. "No, not scared. Just cautious."

"I promise you, we'll be all right. The coastline here is free of dangerous currents. Besides, the sky above us is blue and the weather, calm." Jeb's hands rested on the hull of the small fishing boat as he slid it into the water. "Come on. Climb in. We'll catch a few fish and be back in no time."

Kofi reluctantly climbed into the boat. Jeb followed suit.

The boys rowed out into the deep and cast their fishing rods into the now churning water. The blue sky overhead turned into dark shades of gray, while a gust of wind rocked the tiny boat.

"Jeb, we need to turn around now, before the storm overtakes us."

"But we've got to catch at least one fish before we go back."

"Jeb, please. Let's turn back now."

The waves swelled, violently rocking the tiny boat.

Maybe Kofi was right. Maybe they should go back. Taking the helm, Jeb cast his oar starboard and rowed fiercely toward shore, struggling to keep the tiny craft afloat as the waves swelled higher and higher, pounding against them and crashing over the tiny craft.

Jeb glanced behind him. "Kofi, are you all right?"

Kofi nodded while he frantically rowed on the port side of the tiny craft.

Through the raging wind, Jeb's gaze fell on the shoreline. Only a little farther and they'd reach land. He rowed harder and harder, gasping to catch his breath after every gigantic tidal onslaught.

But suddenly, a huge wave overwhelmed the little boat, capsizing it.

Jeb struggled to cling to the bow while searching frantically for Kofi. "Kofi! Kofi! Where are you?"

He caught a glimpse of his friend hanging desperately onto the stern. "Kofi, hang on to the boat! Don't let go! I'm coming."

With his hands gripping the tiny vessel, Jeb crept across the edge of the craft to grab hold of Kofi. But just as he reached him, Kofi lost his hold and slipped into the depths of the raging waters. Jeb watched in horror as the ocean swallowed his best friend, dragging him down into the deep.

Terror seized Jeb's soul. Was he responsible for Kofi's death?

Another enormous wave overwhelmed Jeb and drove him to shore. In excruciating anguish, he collapsed onto the sand and wept bitterly.

Could he have done more to save his best friend?

* * * *

Tori glanced at the kitchen wall clock as she dried the dish Anna had handed her. Six o'clock. Christmas Eve. How awful to have to spend it without Jeb!

She swallowed the lump in her throat. By now, he should have arrived at his mother's house in Ghana. He'd been gone only since yesterday, and already she missed him terribly.

Did he miss *her?*

She'd hardly slept the night before, thinking about him as he crossed the vast Atlantic Ocean to a strange and distant land.

So far away from her in body. Yet, so close to her in spirit.

Did he feel the same way about her?

Fear nagged relentlessly at her. She'd been tormented with the thought that Jeb didn't love her in the same way she loved him. That to him, their relationship was just a good friendship. Nothing more. That Jeb would have little trouble returning to Ghana and never seeing her again.

Her soul trembled as she took another dish from Anna. Night had already fallen over Philadelphia. Through the kitchen window over the sink, she caught glimpses of the brightly decorated houses on her street, while from the record player in the living room, Christmas songs filtered into the kitchen.

Her heart sank. While everyone celebrated Christmas with loved ones, she would be far from the one she loved most.

Anna handed her another dish to dry. "You seem to be in another world."

"I am. My mind is in Ghana."

Anna glanced at her and smiled. "I wonder why."

Tori could contain her feelings no longer. "Oh, Anna. I miss him so much!"

"Of course, you do. Why wouldn't you?" Anna placed another dish on the dish rack. "He'll be back."

Tori sighed. "I hope so."

Anna paused and looked at Tori. "What do you mean you *hope* so?"

Tori placed the dried dish in the cupboard and took another one from the dish rack. "The tribal elders may not allow him to return to finish his studies."

Anna let out a low whistle. "Oh. I didn't know that."

"If they don't, he'll have to remain in Ghana, and I may never see him again." A shudder ran through Tori at the unfathomable thought.

Anna shook her head. "That would not be good." She pensively resumed her washing.

"No, it wouldn't be good at all." Dare Tori tell Anna the rest? "But worse than that, when Jeb becomes chief, the elders will choose a wife for him from among the tribal women. It's their custom." Her throat hitched.

Her eyes wide, Anna jerked her head toward her sister. "Are you serious?"

"Yes. I couldn't be more serious." Tori's stomach clenched. "Nor more worried."

"But that doesn't seem right. What if a chief doesn't love the woman chosen for him? Why should he be forced to marry her? Seems to me he could do what he wants since he's the chief."

"Seems that way to me, too. But, from what Jeb told me, a chief is not a dictator. He has to consider the wishes of his tribe, especially of his tribal elders."

"Consider, yes. But does he have to go along with those wishes?"

"I guess he could refuse. But if he did, the tribe might find another chief."

Anna faced Tori. "So, are you saying that if Jeb refuses to marry the woman the elders choose for him, he might have to forfeit the chieftaincy?"

"Yes. That's exactly what I'm saying." Tori's jaw tightened. "Jeb might be forced to choose between me and being the chief of his tribe."

"Well, that puts your concern in an entirely different light."

Tori nodded, her muscles tensing. "But there's more, Anna."

Anna paused, holding a sudsy dish in her hand. "More?"

"Yes. My last conversation with Jeb at the airport was not what I'd hoped for."

"What do you mean?"

"He seemed reluctant to make any commitment to me. It was almost as though he were saying goodbye for the last time."

"Are you sure you're not imagining this?"

"I'm sure. I know Jeb, and he wasn't himself."

"Well, of course not. He just lost his father. What do you expect?"

"It was more than that. He acted as though his feelings toward me had cooled. As though Ghana were tugging at his heartstrings, wrenching him from me."

Tori blinked back hot tears. "He seemed as though he'd finally realized what he really wanted in life." She choked on the words. "And it wasn't a relationship with me."

"Tori, I think you're letting your imagination run wild. Why not wait and see how things play out. Jeb has a lot of concerns on his mind right now."

"Yes, I agree. But I don't seem to be one of them."

Anna rinsed the suds off the dish and handed it to Tori to dry. "I think you're getting yourself all worked up over nothing." She smiled. "You have a habit of doing that, you know."

"I hope you're right. But I have this nagging feeling that you're not."

Tori's heart squeezed. What if the situation came down to one choice? Would Jeb choose her over the chieftaincy? Was it selfish of her to hope that? What if, now that he was home, he was drawn back into the ways of his people and forgot her?

Perhaps Jeb didn't really love her but only thought he loved her. Sometimes when people were far away from home, they got caught up in the glamour and excitement of a new culture and new people. Sometimes they were drawn by what was different simply because it *was* different. Not the same, routine life to which they were accustomed.

Sometimes, in the allure of the new, they confused fantasy with reality.

Maybe that's what had happened to Jeb. America was not his homeland. America was different. Exciting.

New.

Maybe this very newness and excitement had swept him off his feet. Clouded his thinking. Thrown his emotions off balance.

Top that off with dating a white woman, and no wonder Jeb felt conflicted. No wonder he wasn't sure about their relationship. No wonder he'd hadn't been able to make a commitment to her at the airport.

Would he ever be able to?

She pushed the frightening thought out of her mind. *One thing at a time, Tori. One thing at a time.* Her mind was running away with her. She had to stop it before she got caught up in a panic.

Anna was right. She mustn't get herself all worked up. It would do no good.

The dishes done, Tori went to her room to finish wrapping presents to keep her mind off Jeb. It didn't work. Around and around, those same three questions whirled in her mind. Would he be permitted to return to the States to finish his studies? Would he be compelled to remain in Ghana?

Worst of all, would he have to marry a woman from his tribe in order to become chief?

The disturbing, obsessive thoughts would not let her go. When she couldn't stand the mental torment any longer, she pulled out a sheet of linen stationery from the top drawer of her desk, refilled her fountain pen, and began to write a letter to Jeb.

Dear Jeb,

I know our last moments together were not what we'd hoped. Or, at least, not what I had hoped. Yet, I care for you too much not to fight for us.

You've been gone only one day and already I miss you terribly. I can't wait until you return. If you do return.

I hope you are well and had a good flight. By now, you have most likely reached your hometown. Your family must be so glad to have you with them again after two long years of absence. I know that you will be a great comfort to them during this time of grieving.

I wish I were there to comfort you. I will keep you and your family in prayer. I hope we will be together again soon, if it is the Lord's will.

Tori held her fountain pen in mid-air, pondering what to say next, if anything. No. Better not to say anything more, despite the emotions churning in her heart, longing to be expressed. Better to leave well enough alone.

She paused. How should she sign the letter? *Love, Tori?* No. That would be too much, given their parting at the airport. *Your friend, Tori?* Too superficial to express the feelings she felt. *Affectionately, Tori.* Yes, that was it.

She signed the letter and carefully copied the address Jeb had given her onto the envelope. Then she placed the letter in her purse. Tomorrow, on her way to class, she would stop at the post office to mail it.

But before doing so, she would seal the letter with a kiss.

And hope that she had not written it in vain.

Chapter 5

Like a painful arrow, anguish pierced Jeb's soul as he passed a sign that read: "Busua, 45 km." It had been ten years since the accident, but he still could not forgive himself. He should have never pressed Kofi to go fishing when his friend had not wanted to go. He should never have launched out to sea without life jackets, despite the fact that both he and Kofi were excellent swimmers.

He should never have been the one to survive, if only for the fact that the blame for going out that day lay at his feet.

Jeb broke out in a cold sweat. Something had died in him that day. And that part of him could never be restored. It had left a gaping hole in his heart that nothing or no one could fill. The worst of it had been breaking the tragic news to Kofi's parents. Their grief-stricken faces had left an indelible mark on Jeb's soul, causing sleepless nights, tormenting dreams, and gut-eating anxiety whenever he ran across them in his hometown. Had the tragic death of her son caused Kofi's mother to die of a broken heart only a short time later? To this day, Jeb grieved at the memory of it all.

Not even with Tori had he shared his anguish. After all, what could she do? What could anyone do? The past was the past. But as much as he wanted to let it lie, he couldn't.

As the city lights of Sekondi-Takoradi appeared in the distance, Jeb forced his thoughts back to the purpose of his visit—to bury his father and to assume leadership of the tribe. The days ahead promised more tension as he dealt with the details of his father's funeral, burial, and Jeb's own appearance and questioning before the tribal elders. Although he was in line to succeed his father as chief, his installation was not assured until the elders had stringently examined his qualifications and approved of them. Topmost on the list was courage.

Jeb swallowed hard. If the elders knew the truth, he'd already failed in that category.

By the time Jeb reached his boyhood house, he needed sleep badly. But he couldn't go to bed yet. He whispered a prayer for strength to carry out his responsibilities as the eldest son of his deceased father.

As he entered the house, the sound of the customary wailing for the dead reached his ears, reinforcing the bitter reality of his father's death. Jeb choked back the sob that stung his throat.

The spacious room was dim, lit only by a single lamp on an end table. An electric fan stood in the corner, casting a slight breeze that barely lifted the oppressive humidity that hung in the air. In the middle of the room, a brightly colored carpet covered a white porcelain-tiled floor. Atop the rug stood a mahogany table with a wreath of red roses lying on it, a tribute to the deceased chief.

Jeb found his mother sitting in a large, cushioned bamboo chair, her face worn, her aged hands kneading a crumpled handkerchief. She wept profusely, shaking her head in disbelief. Surrounding her sat Jeb's aunts, uncles, and cousins. The elders of the tribe were also there. All of them had come to mourn with the grieving family and to pay their respects to Jeb's father.

To his mother's left sat Adofo, Jeb's younger brother, his face a blank stare. Jeb acknowledged him with a nod and, out of respect, proceeded to greet his mother first.

As Jeb approached her, she let out a loud cry and reached for him. "Jebuni!"

"*Ena!*" He greeted her in his native tongue.

He knelt before her and embraced her. "*Ena*, I have come home." In the two long years he'd been gone, Mama had aged quite a bit. Her dark-brown hair had turned to a soft gray, and wrinkles now framed her deep, sad eyes.

"Thank the Lord! I have been eagerly awaiting you." She drew him into a tight embrace and held him for a long moment. Then, gently releasing him, she pointed toward an adjacent room. "Your father's body is in the next room." Jeb's mother always chose her words carefully. She understood that her husband, a Christian, was now with the Lord Jesus Christ. Only his body remained on earth.

As was the tribal custom, the body of a deceased chief remained at his home for the pre-burial mourning period, after which it lay in state in the town hall before being laid to rest in the royal cemetery.

Jeb nodded and then made the rounds of greeting his family. First, his younger brother Adofo, and then his aunts and uncles. Finally, the tribal elders. They treated him with a different kind of respect now that his father had died. Intuitively, they seemed to grasp that Jeb was now their chief, even though they had not yet officially installed him.

Jeb shook their hands and graciously accepted their condolences. He then took a deep breath. It was now time to pay his respects to his father lying in the next room.

* * * *

Both grief and dread were Jeb's twin companions as he entered the large room where his father lay. Jeb's heart ached with the prospect of seeing the lifeless body of his beloved papa.

The room was empty except for the ornately crafted coffin that sat on a bier in the center of it. The coffin was made of mahogany and depicted scenes from the tribe's history. The recently adopted national flag of Ghana, with its red, yellow, and green horizontal stripes punctuated by a black star in the center, stood at the head of the bier. At its foot stood a tribal flag, with its primitive figures and drawings depicting the various occupations of the people of Jeb's tribe.

His father's body was officially dressed in the traditional garb of a Ghanaian chieftain. The colorful garment of gold, burgundy, and green *kente* royal cloth was wrapped around him. The pattern of the garment had the name *Nyankonton*, meaning *God's eyebrow*, and signified the rainbow of God's covenant with man. The cloth symbolized God's beauty, gracefulness, divine creativity, and blessing. Jeb's father had chosen it as his official garb at the beginning of his chieftaincy, determined to live and rule by what it represented. A wide, gold band adorned his right wrist, and chains of gold draped his neck.

The day after Christmas, the body would be removed to the town hall in the village square. There, the people of the village would come and pay their final respects to the man who had served them for many years, and served them well.

His fists curled tight at his sides, Jeb slowly approached the bier. He blinked back the stinging tears that welled up in his tired eyes. But upon seeing his father's body, regally laid out, Jeb broke down and wept. All of his pent-up anguish poured out from his broken heart at this moment of brutal confrontation with the death of the man he adored. The man who had shaped him in the wisdom of life. Guided him through its storms. Trained him and groomed him to be the next chief and taught him how to love God and family and country.

Jeb stood reverently in front of his father's body, gazing at the lifeless figure of the man who had been his hero.

Jeb would sorely miss him.

"*Agya*, I'm home." A sob choked Jeb's words as a torrent of tears flowed from his eyes.

He stood beside the man whose shoes he would soon have to fill. Papa's face was peaceful, serene.

But dead.

Jeb's shoulders shook with grief. No longer would he hear his father say, "Welcome home, son!" No longer would he feel his father's arms wrapped around his shoulders, encouraging him during a difficult time. Never again would Jeb sit at the feet of this man of integrity, honor, and courage, learning from his wisdom and experience.

At the despairing thought, Jeb fell on his father's chest and wept bitterly.

He wept for a long time. When he had exhausted his tears, he rose. Clasping his hands in front of him, he bowed his head and prayed. He prayed in thanksgiving for having had a father who loved him and taught him the ways of God. He prayed for his mother, whose life would radically change now that her husband had died. He prayed for his brother who, at too young an age, had lost his magnificent mentor and role model. He prayed for himself, to whom it now fell to pick up the baton and move forward in his father's footsteps. Footsteps no one could walk in as his father had walked in them. What if Jeb fell short? What if his people did not accept him as they had accepted his father?

What if he failed to uphold his family's royal legacy as it deserved to be upheld?

Jeb shuddered as thought after negative thought bombarded his mind.

He swallowed hard. The weight of the responsibility that had now fallen on his shoulders overwhelmed him. More so because it had fallen upon him so unexpectedly. Not even the outstanding education he'd received provided him any relief from anxiety. Now, more than ever, he needed God's guidance.

He had many pressing decisions to make. Although he hoped to the contrary, he would most likely have to abandon his studies and return home. He would have to deal with transitioning the tribe to his new leadership, seeking to maintain its traditional identity, while doing things differently in order to move the people into a new era. A modern era.

An era of freedom from prejudice, poverty, and illiteracy.

Tori's face flashed across his mind. He needed her now more than ever. He needed her at his side to encourage him, support him, and sustain him. To share in his work.

To love him.

But his family would never approve of his marrying a white woman—especially not now that he was to become chief. Despite the influence of Christianity upon his people, racism still held a powerful sway over them. Traditions died hard. Changing those traditions would require much patience, time, and effort.

But regarding Tori, there was no time. His only hope would be to marry her before the tribe chose his wife for him. Before the tribe learned of his love for her.

Before he lost her to another man.

Jeb shuddered. Would he be constrained to marry Tori without the tribe's knowledge or permission? Doing so seemed the only solution to his dilemma—and yet such a choice could mean death to his chieftaincy. The elders would interpret it as an act of betrayal. An insult to their wisdom. A blow to their centuries-old tradition.

Guilt pricked him. He was not one to deceive in any manner. Yet, if he told the tribal elders that he wanted to marry a white woman, they would find another chief. Not that Jeb desired the chieftaincy for himself. No! He desired it to fulfill his father's mandate. His expectations.

His legacy.

To forfeit the chieftaincy for the love of a white woman would be to betray his papa. And for that, Jeb could never forgive himself. Yet, to give up Tori would be to betray his heart, and hers as well. And he could never forgive himself for that, either. Without Tori as his wife, he would be a chief without hope. A chief without joy.

A chief without heart.

With her at his side, he would be a chief by birth, but a chief without a stool.

The enormous weight of the decision overwhelmed him. For now, he would put it aside. He needed to focus on getting through the funeral and settling his father's affairs. Until then, he would wait on God to discern His will.

Jeb gave a slight bow to his father's body and then left the room. He returned to his mother in the living room and sat down next to her in a chair that had been provided for him. It was time to discuss his father's funeral arrangements and who would be selected as chief mourner.

The funeral service was set for December 27th. There was much to be done, the most important of which was to write to Tori. She would be wondering how he was and what was going on.

He could tell her how he was.

But as for what was going on, he himself wished he knew.

* * * *

The day after Christmas, Tori sat in the tiny library carrel where she'd sequestered herself for the afternoon to study for her final exams. Jeb had been gone a few days, but it seemed like an eternity.

The library carrel had become her personal, private oasis. Her home away from home. The place she went to when she needed to clear her mind or find peace for her soul.

And now that Jeb was gone, the carrel had become the place where she went to dream about his return. She loved the quiet nook tucked away on the fourth floor of the expansive library, just behind the stacks and stacks of art books that inspired her just by looking at the titles on their spines. The old, musty tomes enveloped her like a warm security blanket, providing stability to her otherwise rocky world.

This carrel—*her* carrel—had become the hiding place that protected her from the cold stares and cruel remarks that had assailed her almost daily since she'd started dating Jeb. It had become her place of refuge and escape from the increasingly vicious prejudice surrounding her deepening relationship with the man she loved.

Ever since she'd started dating Jeb, the subtle innuendoes had not escaped Tori's notice. Nor had the ugly, under-the-breath slurs—from both male and female students alike—as she walked down the hallways between classes, grabbed a sandwich in the cafeteria, or hurried across campus from one building to another.

Not for the first time, she wondered if this was what Jeb had endured all of his life in apartheid Africa. If so, how did he withstand it? Would she be able to endure it should they end up getting married?

Married? Why did she think that was even a possibility at this point?

Tori gazed out the large, Romanesque window that over-looked the campus. The barrenness of the late December landscape reflected the barrenness of her heart without Jeb. Patches of snow dotted the brown, grassless lawn. Bare-limbed beech trees, their branches swaying in the light wind, sang the mournful dirge of a dreary winter day. Above, the pale, blue-white sky portended a snowstorm.

Would it always be winter in her heart?

Would springtime ever come?

She reluctantly returned to the pile of books in front of her. In three short weeks, pending the passing of her exams, she'd complete her penultimate semester. One more to go—and then graduation in May. She'd finish with a Master of Arts degree in Art History. The culmination of a long, arduous journey—not only academic, but also emotional. The life of art for which she'd prepared would now become a reality.

She'd already accepted a position as assistant art director at a major magazine publishing house in the city. Quite a feat for a pending graduate. She was finally on her way.

But what did it mean to be *on one's way*?

One's way to what?

Yes, a good career lay before her. But a good career could not satisfy her deepest longing for love. For significance.

For acceptance.

She'd accomplished much. But would her father now recognize her worth? Would he now approve of her and accept her?

If the past were any indication, Pop would never change his opinion of her. She'd have to spend the rest of her life living with the stigma of being an annoyance to him. An unwanted child.

An accident.

Why couldn't he look on her as a bonus blessing instead?

She swallowed the painful lump that always rose to her throat whenever her father came to mind. No matter what she did, she could never please him. Why even try any longer?

Jeb was different. She hadn't failed to please him. He accepted her. Encouraged her. Made her feel worthwhile.

Yet, what if Jeb's feelings toward her had changed? What if he were drifting away from her?

What if he discovered she wasn't all he'd thought she was?

What if? What if? What if? Tori grabbed her head with both hands to drive out the distressing questions.

"Got a headache?"

A familiar voice interrupted Tori's racing thoughts. She looked up.

"Hi, Sue. No. No headache. Just a bunch of worrisome thoughts."

"Been there. No fun." Susanna Durgan, one of Tori's classmates, leaned over the edge of the carrel. "How's it going?"

Tori managed a smile. "I'm cramming for my last final. Can't wait till the semester is over."

"I hear you. I have two more exams and am working on fumes. I pulled an all-nighter for my most recent exam and might have to for this next one, too."

Tori laughed. "I tried that once and flunked the exam. I'm a mess without sleep."

Susanna changed the subject. "Hey, Tori." A question laced her words.

"Yes?"

Susanna glanced around and then focused her gaze on Tori. "I'm telling you this as a friend, but there's talk around campus about you and that colored guy you're dating."

Tori's muscles stiffened. "And?"

"And—" Susanna hedged. "I don't know. Just wanted to warn you, I guess."

Tori's senses went on high alert. "Warn me about what?"

"About what's going on behind your back."

Tori stood, her jaw tightening. "I know what's going on behind my back. I've heard the slurs. I've heard the murmurs. And, frankly, I don't care."

Susanna frowned, concern written in her eyes. "It could get ugly, Tori."

An alarm shot through Tori's soul. "What do you mean 'ugly'?"

Susanna hesitated. "Ugly—as in hurtful." Her gaze locked knowingly with Tori's. "Harmful, even."

Tori stiffened. So it had come to this. To physical threats.

If only Jeb were here.

Tori sighed. "I guess I should thank you for the warning."

"That's all it was, Tori. A warning. Nothing more. I personally have no problem with your dating Jeb." Susanna smiled. "Frankly, I admire your courage."

"Thanks, Sue. You're a good friend." Tori smiled. "And a genuine one."

"Thanks." Susanna gave her a hug. "Well, I'll leave you to your studying. I've got a class in ten minutes." With that, she left.

Tori heaved a sigh and sank back down into her chair. Again she wondered: Was this what she and Jeb would have to endure for the rest of their lives if they ended up getting married? Would they forever be the object of wagging tongues and wicked hearts?

She returned to her books. No matter. Let the tongues wag and the hearts be wicked. As for Tori Pendola, no one would stand in her way. She would follow Jeb Kalitsi to the ends of the earth.

If only he would let her.

Chapter 6

"You dirty—!" The offensive racial epithet, followed by a sudden splash of spittle on her face, struck Tori like a bomb, sending her reeling as she walked across a solitary stretch of campus.

She looked up into her assailant' face and recognized him as a classmate. He was white, tall, and mean-looking.

"How dare you?" Fire rushed to her face as she wiped off the spittle with the back of her hand.

He came up closer. "How dare I?" He grabbed her wrist and jerked her. "Do you really want to know?"

She broke loose from his grip, her heart pounding. "I'll have you arrested on charges of assault and battery!"

His face was in hers. "Oh, you will, will you? Just try it and see what happens. I'd think twice before reporting me to the police."

Tori's blood turned to ice. Was it an empty threat? Or could he make good on it?

The young man sneered, gave her a sinister, triumphant grin, and walked away.

Sick inside, Tori took a handkerchief from her purse and further wiped the disgusting spittle off her face. So this was what Susanna had meant when she'd warned that things could become ugly.

Shaken to the core, Tori skipped her next class and headed home. What could possess a person to harbor such bitter hatred against someone simply because of his skin color? It made no sense.

If only Jeb were here! But maybe it was better he wasn't. He'd be furious over what had happened to her and might take matters into his own hands. Not a good thing for a foreign-exchange student who wasn't a citizen of the United States. Nor for a man destined to be the chief of his tribe.

As Tori hurried to the bus stop, she kept looking over her shoulder. Was she being followed? Were others besides that young man this upset about her dating a black man? Or had the young man acted alone?

She gasped for breath. Would she have to put up with this for the rest of her life if she married Jeb? Most likely, yes.

But she'd be honored to do it because she loved him.

Her mind raced to her parents. Should she tell them about what had happened? If she did, they'd find out she'd been dating a black man. Then what? They'd disown her for sure.

But if she didn't tell them—. She caught her breath. She would tell Anna. Anna knew Jeb, and level-headed Anna would know exactly what to do.

Tori approached the bus stop. The late-December temperature had dropped to freezing, and the sun was low in the western sky. Soon it would drop neatly into the horizon. In the distance, the downtown buildings turned on their lights. Darkness fell early in Philadelphia in winter.

But today, darkness had come to her soul.

She shuddered.

A small group of students waited for the bus to arrive. They chatted happily, oblivious to the turmoil in Tori's heart. She joined them, feeling safe in their midst. As long as she remained hidden in the crowd, she'd be all right. The young man couldn't find her there. And, if he did, there were others around her to protect her. Only when she was alone would she have to be extra careful, lest the young man appear yet again to harass her.

After several moments, the bus pulled up against the curb, and Tori boarded with the others. Still trembling, she found a seat in the back, hoping to keep a watchful eye on the passengers in front of her and on her surroundings.

The ride was uneventful, and soon the bus deposited her at her stop. She descended the three steps onto the sidewalk, looked around her, and then ran the one block to her house. Out of breath, she put her key into the lock, turned the knob, and entered. Not until she'd shut the door securely behind her did she exhale the long breath she'd been holding.

Safely home at last!

Her legs went limp.

"Tori, is that you?" Mom's voice came from the kitchen.

"Yes, Mom."

In an instant, Mom was at the front door. "What are you doing home so early? I thought you had a class this afternoon."

"I do." She caught her breath. "I mean, I did."

"Then why aren't you in it?"

Should she tell Mom what happened?

"Is Anna home?"

"No, she and Pop are at the office. They'll be home in time for dinner."

Tori had wanted to speak only with Anna.

"Tori, are you all right?"

Tori had never been good at hiding her feelings, nor had Mom ever been bad at reading them.

"Let's sit down, Mom. There's something important I have to tell you."

Concern crossed her mother's face. "All right." She removed her apron and hung it on the bottom post of the bannister.

Tori sat on the sofa while Mom sat in Pop's recliner. Her mother folded her hands, waiting for Tori to begin.

But as soon as Tori opened her mouth, the words caught in her throat. As much as she tried, she could not speak the truth that would forever alter Mom's life.

Mama leaned forward. "Tori, what is it? You look pale, as though you've just had a great fright."

Tori forced herself to gather the words. "I have."

* * * *

It was dark when Jeb, Adofo, and Mama finally arrived home from the funeral. The day had been long and wearisome. His father's funeral celebration had gone on longer than usual, with much dancing and feasting, as was the custom in Ghana, especially at the funeral of a chief.

Adofo bid Mama and Jeb goodnight and returned to his own home nearby while Jeb sat with Mama. As they drank tea at the kitchen table, his mother got right down to business.

"Jebuni, it is your duty now to take over the chieftaincy of the tribe. From your childhood, your father has been preparing you for this moment."

Jeb nodded. "Yes, but I never thought it would arrive so soon." He sighed. "Nor, truthfully, do I know where to begin."

She placed a hand on his. "The tribal elders will guide you. The tribe will require your leadership immediately. You must return to Ghana, my son."

"But what about my studies?"

"You may have to abandon them. Unless, of course, the tribe is willing to appoint an interim chief until you return. But, I doubt that very much. There is no one capable of assuming the position better than you. Moreover, it is your duty as your father's son. You were born into it."

Indeed, he had been. His father had ingrained that truth in Jeb's soul throughout his life. The chief was chief by birth. It was Jeb's duty to assume the position and to carry on his father's legacy. One day, Jeb would pass it on to his own son.

He rested his elbows on the arms of the straight-backed chair and folded his hands. "What will happen first?"

"The tribal elders will interview you to ensure that you are qualified for the position. Once you pass the interview, you will be installed as chief."

Jeb's muscles tightened. What if the tribal elders discovered he wasn't qualified?

"Afterward, the tribe will soon choose a wife for you to be your help and support as you fulfill your duties to the tribe."

Jeb's stomach clenched. He hadn't planned on telling Mama about Tori just yet. But perhaps he should before things progressed too far.

"Mama, there is something I must tell you."

"What is it, my son?"

He hesitated. "I have met an American woman and …" He took a breath and then voiced the directive of his heart. "I want to marry her." Jeb took in a quick breath. "And you may as well know now that she is white."

Mama paled. "You would dare add more grief to the grief of burying your father?" She squared her jaw. "How could you betray your father's memory in such a way? You know it is your duty to marry a woman from our tribe. The elders will choose the one best suited to serve at your side."

"But the woman I love is perfectly suited to me. And she will be suited to the tribe as well."

Mama rose and leaned over Jeb. "No woman outside our tribe is suited to be the wife of the chief! Especially not a white woman!" She narrowed her eyes. "If your father had known this would happen, he would have never sent you to America." She pointed an index finger at him. "I am thankful he did not live to witness your betrayal." She then turned away and paced the floor.

The words stung deeply, slicing into the very depths of Jeb's heart.

"I love her, Mama. I cannot live without her."

She stopped and turned toward him. "A chief must place God's will before love! Your father's own words."

"But I believe she *is* God's will for me, Mama. I cannot marry a woman from our tribe. I love Tori more than life itself, and I intend to marry her and bring her back to Ghana. The people will eventually accept her and grow to love her."

"You deceive yourself, my son. Tradition must and will prevail."

Jeb's insides roiled. His own mother, who had always supported him, seemed to be turning her back on him. "Perhaps we should continue this conversation at another time. A time when our emotions are under better control and reason has taken over."

She dismissed him with a wave of her hand. "As far as I am concerned, the conversation is over. I have nothing more to say to you."

"Mama, listen. We are both tired and grieving and need rest."

"From now on, I will have no rest. The firstborn son of my womb is a traitor. He has betrayed me and betrayed his people. This is a death far worse than your father's."

Her hurtful words smashed Jeb's soul into a pulp.

Mama stood before him, her frail frame trembling. "Of one thing you can be sure. If you do not marry a woman from our tribe, you will not be approved by the elders, and that would break my heart."

"Mama, you are forcing me to choose between the chief-taincy and the woman I love."

"Precisely. It is a choice you will have to make. And the sooner you make it, the better."

His mother was being unjust. But, honorable son that he was, he would never disrespect her in any way. "Mama, I understand that you are angry and disappointed. That this news of mine has taken you by surprise. But time will prove that what I am saying about Tori is true. She is a good woman, Mama. She will love you like a daughter."

Mama raised her chin. "I will never accept a woman outside the tribe as my daughter, especially a white woman!" Then, turning abruptly, she left the room.

Jeb's head spun. Mama had thrown down the gauntlet. Would he pick it up and fight for his chiefdom? Would he fight for Tori, the woman he loved?

Or would he let the gauntlet lie, turn away, and leave Ghana forever behind?

* * * *

Tori sat on the edge of the sofa in the living room and composed herself as best she could. "Mom, I've been meaning to tell you something for quite a while now, but it's never been the right time."

Her mother sat across from Tori and listened intently, a concerned look on her face.

"But now is the right time." Tori gathered her thoughts. "For the past several weeks, I've been dating a young man I really like. His name is Jeb."

"So, that's where you've been so many evenings a week."

Tori nodded. "Jeb is an exchange student at Penn, and he's from Ghana."

Worry dawned in Mom's eyes. "Ghana? Do you mean … Is he black?"

Tori braced herself for the worst. "Yes. He's black."

Mom lowered her head and wrung her hands. "I see."

Tori's face grew hot. "*What* do you see, Mom?

Her mother raised her head and narrowed her eyes. "I see that your father is not going to like this one bit."

Tori's muscles stiffened. "What about you?"

Mom hesitated. "Let me just say that I personally think your father is going too far with his prejudice, but I do understand his concern about the mixed-race children you would have if you married a black man. Your children would belong to neither race."

Tori squared her jaw. "Mom, there's only one race. The human race."

Mom sighed. "While that is true, society does not recognize that truth."

Tori stood. "So, should I live my life based on what society thinks or based on the truth?"

"Tori, we have to live in the real world. No matter what the truth is, mixed-race children are rejected by both blacks and whites. They live in limbo and face many struggles in life that all-blacks or all-whites do not face. The reality of life is that people are judged on the color of their skin."

"And that's disgusting to me!" Tori paced the room. "Who are people to judge, anyway? Only God can judge, and He judges not on skin color but on heart attitude."

Her eyes wide, Mom looked up at Tori. "It's not a sin for your father and me to be concerned about our future grandchildren."

"Mom, you're twisting things. Are you really concerned about your future grandchildren? Or are you more concerned about your own reputation?"

Mom drew back, a stunned but guilty expression on her face. "Tori, look. I'm just trying to warn you. If you continue in your relationship with this black man, you will face difficult challenges that other couples do not face."

Her mother was right in that respect. Just that very day, Tori had faced a difficult challenge she would not have faced had Jeb been white. That challenge was exactly the purpose of her present conversation with her mother.

"I know. I've already faced one of those challenges." Tori sat down on the sofa again. "That's what this conversation is about."

Mom folded her hands in her lap.

Tori swallowed hard. "This evening, as I was leaving the library, I was assaulted."

Mom gasped. "Oh, my! Are you all right? What happened?"

Tori proceeded to tell her mother about the student who had called her a derogatory name, grabbed her by the wrist, and threatened her if she didn't stop dating Jeb. "I didn't want to tell you about this, but I couldn't keep it from you. Frankly, I'm very worried."

"As well you should be. Have you notified the police?"

Tori shook her head. "No."

"Then I think you need to right away."

"But the assailant warned me that if I report him, he'll make good on the threat."

Mom's face grew pale. "I knew something like this would happen if you dated a black man." She bit her lip. "I'm sure your father will want you to call the police."

"What about the threat?'

Mom's eyes narrowed. "You should have thought of that before dating that colored man."

Tori winced.

"We'll just have to wait until your father gets home. He'll know what to do."

"What we need to do is whatever it takes to stop prejudice in the first place."

"Tori, you can't do anything to stop prejudice. You just have to live with it. You will either have to break off your relationship with Jeb or live with this kind of harassment for the rest of your life."

"No. I don't have to live with it, Mom. And I can do something to change it."

Mom sighed. "Tori, you're fighting a giant bigger than you."

"Yes, that may be so. But the giant is not bigger than God."

Mom shook her head and stood. Her gaze softened as she stopped in front of Tori. "When I was your age, I, too, was idealistic. But life taught me a few things. Maybe life will have to teach you a few things as well." She sighed. "The hard way."

Tori shuddered. What did her mother mean by "the hard way"? Where would the "hard way" lead?

Was Tori willing to go that way?

Mom sighed. "I'd better go start dinner. Your father will be home soon. And he won't be too happy when he hears what you've just told me." She paused. "In fact, brace yourself, Tori, because your father will be furious."

Tori sank back down onto the sofa. Her head spun. Her mind raced. It was bad enough facing an assailant.

But nothing could be worse than facing her father's wrath.

Chapter 7

Tori hardly ate during dinner. Thankfully, her mother had not mentioned anything to Pop of the assault injury. That would remain for Tori to tell him later.

After dinner, Tori had the opportunity to discuss the assault with Anna.

"I'd suggest you play it down, make it low key. Pop will explode when you tell him you're dating a black man. When he learns about the assault, he'll explode even more.

"But, Anna, how can I downplay something so serious?"

"I'm not denying it's serious. But it could get more serious if Pop takes matters into his own hands." Anna sighed. "Which, knowing Pop, I'm afraid he will. Then things would get really bad."

Tori pondered Anna's words. What Tori didn't want to do at any cost was to complicate matters even more. They were complicated enough as they were.

She went into the living room where Pop was reading the newspaper. "Pop, may I talk with you for a moment?"

He scowled.

Not a good sign.

"Okay. But only for a moment. I gotta catch up on the news, you know."

Tori sat on the sofa opposite Pop's recliner. "Pop, something happened today that I think you should know about."

He folded his arms across his chest. "Go ahead."

She blurted the words. "I was assaulted on campus."

Pop unfolded his arms and sat forward, his face contorting. "What?" His voice boomed. "Who's the scoundrel? I'll kill him with my own hands."

While thankful for Pop's protective instinct, Tori worried about his vengeance. "He's a student in one of my classes."

"Why did he assault you?"

The moment Tori had dreaded for a long time had arrived. "Because I'm dating a black man."

Pop flew out of his recliner. "You're what?" He towered above her.

A shiver ran through Tori.

"So, that's what you've been doing night after night? And right under my nose! How dare you date a colored guy when you know how I feel about that!"

"But, Pop, don't you care more that I was assaulted?" The old feelings of rejection gnawed at her yet again.

"You brought it on yourself by dating a black man."

Her father's words sliced her to the core.

He sat back down in his recliner. "Tell me what happened."

Tori told him the whole story. When she got to the part about the threat of harm, Pop's eyes narrowed. "Have you reported this to the university authorities and to the police?"

"No."

"Why not?"

"Because, frankly, I don't know if the student was just spouting empty threats. He warned me that if I reported him, he would carry out his threats." Tori lowered her head.

"Point him out to me, and I'll take good care of him."

"Pop, please. Don't take matters into your own hands. I'm willing to call the police if you think that's the best thing to do."

Pop glared at her. "The best thing to do is to stop dating that colored guy."

Her father's prejudice cut deep. "I can't, Pop."

"Why not?"

"Because I love him."

"You love him? How can you love a guy who puts you in danger?"

Tori refused to take the bait. "Pop, Jeb didn't put me in danger. He's in Ghana visiting his own family." She blinked back stinging tears. "*Prejudice* put me in danger."

Pop shifted in his chair. "Whatever it was, the only thing I know is that my daughter is in danger because she's been dating a black guy." He pointed a warning index finger at her. "I'm telling you, Tori, if you don't break off this relationship now, only more trouble lies ahead for you and, possibly, for all of us. Either you tell this guy to get lost, or I might have to tell you to get lost."

Pop's reckless words knocked the wind out of her. Nausea overwhelmed her. There it was again. The paralyzing feeling of rejection that stifled her breath. Pop would never want her. She'd always be a nuisance to him. Always a reject.

Always an accident.

Pop picked up his newspaper. "I want you to notify your professor, the university authorities, and the police about the assault. Report this student. And the next time you see him, tell him if he lays a hand on you again, he'll have your father to contend with." Pop picked up his newspaper. "Oh, one last thing. Tell him if he comes near this house, I'll welcome him with a shotgun in my hand."

* * * *

The day after his father's funeral, Jeb awakened to the morning trill of the purple, glossy starling just outside his bedroom window. The lovely creature sat perched on the branch of a nearby walnut tree, happily welcoming the new day.

Jeb stretched his arms over his head, yawned, and lay in bed for a few moments, thanking the Lord for a new day. What it held, he did not know. What he did know was that he would need God's help to face it.

He spent a few moments in prayer and then rose from his bed to wash and dress. Today he would meet with the tribal elders to be interviewed and, he hoped, approved for the chieftaincy.

He made his way to the kitchen. The house was quiet. No one was around. He opened the door that led to the veranda. There he found his mother sitting in a large wicker chair, staring across the expansive field of tall grass that stood in front of the house. In the distance, dozens of workers, their backs bent, cultivated sugarcane, cassava, and maize.

"Good morning, Mama."

Mama nodded in reply but did not say a word.

"I trust you slept well."

"As well as one can sleep after learning her son is a traitor."

Jeb's stomach churned. A night of rest had only strengthened her bitterness against him.

"Mama, will you be angry with me forever?"

She turned toward him, her eyes aflame. "And longer than that!"

He sat down in the chair next to her. "Mama, please. I want no rift between us."

"It is you alone who have created the rift. It is you alone who can mend it."

Jeb rose. No sense arguing with her. They would just end up going around in circles. Mama was a pure traditionalist. Change was hard for her, as it was for most of the people of his tribe, including the elders. Was there anything he could do to get his mother to relent? To accept the fact that he was, after all, a grown man who could marry whomever he wished, regardless of tribal tradition?

Habit ran deep in a country that had had little exposure to ideas outside itself. Traditions became ingrained, feeding upon themselves, devouring possibilities for growth. According to his mother's historical and cultural paradigm, the tribe had always chosen the chief's wife, and the tribe would always choose the chief's wife. The chief had always had a black wife, so the chief would always have a black wife. Blacks had always married blacks, so blacks would always marry blacks. Plain and simple. What was there to discuss?

But Jeb had plenty to discuss. Several years of living abroad had opened his eyes to new ways of thinking, new ways of living. He'd come to realize that the old ways were not always the best ways, especially when they involved prejudice of any kind. Prejudice cut both ways and had to stop.

But where to begin? If Mama's attitude were any indication, the entire tribe would likely oppose his choice of Tori.

He took a deep breath and braced himself for the worst. "I'm going to get some breakfast."

He left the veranda and went to the kitchen to find something to eat. Normally, Mama would have cooked his favorite, *hausa koko*. But today, she was obviously in no mood to prepare anything for him.

Nor was she in any mood to hold a civil conversation with him.

After a light breakfast of fruit, Jeb returned to the veranda. "I'm going to the village to meet with the elders for the formal interview."

Mama stared straight ahead. "I hope they approve you."

It was the first encouraging thing Mama said since their argument.

"You must tell them that you have already chosen the woman you want to marry and that she is white."

He drew in a deep breath. "I had already planned to do that."

Mama turned toward him. "May the Lord's will be done."

"Amen."

As he drove over the unpaved dirt roads of his village, he surveyed the region from which he'd been absent for two years. Not much had changed. His country was still poor. His people, still uneducated. Men still trudged along dirt roads, leading mules drawing produce-laden carts. Women still worked from morning to night, raising children whose fathers were absent for days at a time, seeking work in other regions to support them.

Jeb sighed. Something needed to be done to change the social and economic climate of his homeland. Current policies would just bring more of the same.

His years of living and studying in America had shown him that the popular vote of the common man was the key to effecting economic and social change in a country. While his tribe espoused voting, the only votes that counted were those of the elders. The common man had no official say in matters that governed him. Nor did the women. Jeb wanted to change that. But dare he present the idea to the elders? Were they ready for it? Surely they would question him on his future policies of government.

He pulled into the large area in front of the tribal meeting place. His was the only car. Few were those in Ghana who owned vehicles. Walking was still the main mode of transportation.

Whispering a prayer for guidance, he entered the town hall where, as a boy, he'd often accompanied his father. The elders had already taken their seats. The interview of a new chief should have been a hopeful time, but no hope informed their faces.

Jeb walked to the center of the large room and stood before them. One by one, he scanned their faces, trying to read them. He knew each one by name. They had been long-time friends of his father. Respected men who had counseled Papa for many years.

As Jeb's gaze covered the group of elders, his heart lurched. On the far right, in the back row, sat Yafeu Adomako, Kofi's father. Recognition brought a rush of guilt, followed by a surge of panic. Would the tragic accident play a part in the elder's decision to vote for Jeb as chief? For a candidate to the stool to have shown himself weak in the face of danger was cause for instant rejection.

Jeb squared his shoulders, took a deep breath, and addressed the men before him. "Greetings, most venerable elders. I am here for the required interview for the chieftaincy."

Elder Siisi Odamtten, the most senior of the elders, motioned to Jeb to sit in the chair that had been placed in the center of the room. Jeb nodded and sat down, putting his hands on his knees to keep his nervousness at bay.

Elder Odamtten spoke first. "Jebuni, we are here to discuss a matter of the gravest concern that directly relates to your inherited position as chief of our tribe."

Jeb fastened his eyes on the speaker.

"As you know, it is the custom of the tribe, among other duties, to choose the new chief's wife from our own tribe before the chief is stooled."

Jeb's muscles tightened. Why had the elder begun with the question of the chief's wife? Why had he not begun with matters of graver importance to the community, like tribal policy?

Jeb cleared his throat. "I have already chosen my wife. And, moreover, she is white."

A united gasp arose from the council.

Elder Odamtten glared at Jeb. "You have dared to defy tribal custom?"

"I have, most respected Elder." Jeb struggled to maintain control of the emotions raging within him.

"Are you aware that such an action on your part could cost you the chieftaincy?"

Protest rose to Jeb's lips, but he restrained it. A chief must never show himself impetuous, but calm and level-headed. He scanned the frozen faces of those sitting before him. "According to tribal tradition, the chieftaincy is mine by birth. No one can take it from me unless I commit a crime."

"That is correct."

"So, may I ask, what crime have I committed? Is it a crime for me to choose my own wife instead of complying with tribal tradition?"

Elder Odamtten sought refuge in the faces of his fellow elders and then turned toward Jeb once again. "You are correct. There is no tribal law that forbids a chief from choosing his own wife, nor from marrying a white woman. But, because of our deeply ingrained traditions, we fear there will be disturbances among the tribesmen."

"How so?"

"We fear an uprising because of the white woman."

Jeb bristled at their disrespectful use of the term, *the white woman*. "Just because she is white does not make her any less of a woman." He regretted the sharp edge to his voice, fearing it would be misinterpreted as rebellion and not defense of his beloved. He softened his tone. "Truly, she is a remarkable woman. I know that, if given a chance, she will capture the hearts of our people."

His plea seemed to go in one ear and out the other.

"You fail to understand the traditions of our people, Jebuni. They do not look well on their chief's marrying outside their tribe, especially to a white woman. You owe it to them to abide by tribal tradition."

"But what if tribal tradition is ill-advised? Archaic? Not in keeping with current cultural and political philosophy?"

"He's been too long in America!" An elder shouted from the second row.

Chief elder Siisi Odamtten took charge. "Dare you question tribal tradition and the wisdom of your elders?"

Jeb bit his tongue. He'd pushed too close to the edge. Better to keep his personal feelings private for the time being. Better to show respect for the men sitting before him. Better to present an attitude of quiet submission while keeping to himself his resolute intention to marry Tori, no matter what.

"I do not question your wisdom, respected elder. Nor do I question tribal tradition. I simply do not totally understand it nor agree with it." Hoping he'd doused their ire, he resolved to choose his words more carefully from now on.

A strong voice rose from the back of the room. Yafeu Adomako stood solemnly, his bitter gaze trained on Jeb. "You ask what crime you have committed?"

All eyes turned toward Kofi's father.

"I say that you have committed a crime far worse than defying tribal tradition." Yafeu paused. "You killed my son!"

Total silence gripped the room. Yafeu's words lingered in the air like the putrid smell of a skunk.

Jeb gasped for air. All the tormenting guilt, remorse, and anguish that had lain buried just beneath the surface of his soul now exploded like molten lava erupting from a volcano. He tightened his jaw, forcing back the searing lump that lodged in the back of his throat.

Suddenly he was back on the little fishing boat as it thrashed against the high waves that beat mercilessly against it. He pushed his oar against the waves, but it was like a small stick trying to tame a vicious lion.

Kofi screamed. "We're going to drown! We're going to drown!"

A high wave overpowered the boat, capsizing it, and plunging them into the raging sea.

Jeb looked for Kofi but could not see him.

"Kofi! Kofi!"

At last, Jeb caught a glimpse of his friend. He reached for him to grab him round the waist. But just as his hand was about to take hold of Kofi's arm, another huge wave enveloped him, tore him from Jeb's grasp, and drove him out to sea.

Overcome by the power of the storm, Jeb felt himself going under as well. But another huge wave overtook him and carried him back to shore.

A cold sweat covered Jeb's forehead. The room spun around him as the faces of the elders melded into a huge blur. Was he going to die? Right here in front of them?

"Are you all right?" The hand of the chief elder standing beside him now rested on Jeb's arm.

Composing himself, Jeb nodded. "Yes. I'm fine, respected elder." Jeb took in a deep breath. "I apologize for the temporary distraction. It won't happen again."

But would it happen again? Would he ever be rid of the guilt? The self-hatred? The self-condemnation? Would he ever be free of the tormenting memory? The recurrent nightmare?

The unrelenting remorse?

Kofi's father pointed at him. "Cowardice is not befitting to a tribal chief. I propose, therefore, that Jebuni Kalitsi not be given the stool."

Yafeu's accusing finger pointed straight at Jeb's heart, like a piercing sword, inflicting a fatal wound on Jeb's soul that was worse than death by any physical wound.

He kept his gaze fixed on Kofi's father. The word *betrayal* pounded in Jeb's mind. This man, who had told Jeb he'd forgiven him, who'd told Jeb that his son's death was not Jeb's fault—this same man was now changing his story and accusing Jeb of his son's death.

How could this be? Never in the past ten years since the accident had Kofi's father brought up the incident. Never had he treated Jeb with disrespect or disdain. On the contrary, he'd been kind and compassionate toward his son's best friend and understanding of Jeb's youth. Had it all been a hoax? A pretense?

A lie?

What was really happening? Had Kofi's father been harboring bitterness all of these years? Was he now using his son's death as an excuse for keeping Jeb from the chieftaincy? But, if so, why?

Did Kofi's father truly think that Jeb would be a threat to the tribe because of his failure to save Kofi's life? It was common knowledge among the tribe that a man with a blemished past could not serve as a good example to his subjects nor command their respect. If it could be proven that Jeb was a man of questionable character, then he would not be enstooled as chief.

His heart bleeding inside, Jeb looked at the elders. All seemed arrayed against him. These same men who, when his father was alive, had encouraged Jeb, supported him, taught him the tribal traditions of leadership had now turned against him.

And for no solid reason.

Until Yafeu's accusation, the main obstacle to his becoming chief had been Tori. Jeb was in love with a white woman and wanted to marry her. The elders considered this rebellion.

What would Papa think if he were still alive? Would he consider his son rebellious for wanting to marry the woman he loved?

No. Papa had taught him to follow his heart. His spirit. His gut.

Jeb's insides hardened. Not only had the tribal elders betrayed him. They'd also betrayed his father.

Jeb smelled mutiny in the ranks.

A shaft of sunlight pierced through an open window and rested on Jeb. Had heaven opened a portal to confirm its will that Jeb be chief? If so, heaven would have to convince the elders of its will.

Chief Odamtten spoke. "It seems as though there are two objections to your ascending to the stool. One is rebellion. You refuse to submit to the tribe's choice of a wife for you. Two, you acted in a cowardly fashion regarding Kofi's death." He paused. "I wish to add a third objection. You desire to marry a white woman."

Ah! There it was. The real reason was Tori. A white woman. A symbol of apartheid's greatest enemy. The other reasons were simply excuses for the real one.

Jeb opened his mouth to protest but thought the better of it. No argument would convince lifelong apartheid proponents that racial prejudice was wrong. Only God could do that.

The chief elder stepped forward. "The tribe will deliberate on these three objections and return its verdict by sundown tonight." He raised his chin. "Jebuni Kalitsi, you are dismissed. You will appear again before this council this evening at sundown for our decision."

Jeb's heart fell to his feet. The examination had been one-sided. No questions about his policies, his philosophy of leadership, his hopes and plans for the tribe. No discussion of what really mattered. Like the future of the tribe. The well-being of the people. The role of the tribe in the larger picture of Ghana.

Nothing.

Nothing but prejudice designed to keep Jeb from fulfilling his rightful place as chief. A place that was his by birth and inheritance. A place that God, he was sure, had ordained for him to fill.

He turned and, without a word, left the town hall and headed toward his rental car.

Not a single elder followed him as he left the interview. He'd hoped at least to have one supporter. But no. All of the elders stood against him.

As he approached his car, the late morning sun beat heavily on his brow, creating shimmering haze that formed a mirage in the air in front of him. How ironic! Maybe his entire chieftaincy was a mirage. An unfounded dream.

A dream that was not meant to be.

Perspiration rolled down his face and into the collar of his shirt. He took a handkerchief from his pocket and wiped his face and neck. Then he entered the car, started the engine, and drove over the bumpy, dirt road toward his mother's house.

His heart sank. His trip to his homeland had turned out to be a nightmare. Not only had Mama turned against him, but now the tribal leaders had also expressed doubt about his qualifications for the chieftaincy. But those doubts had nothing to do with his preparedness and training, which, according to all standards, were superb.

They had everything to do with his choice of a wife.

Gripping the steering wheel, Jeb bristled as he drove home from the meeting with the elders. The injustice of their position gnawed at him. He needed to let it go before it did damage to his soul.

But letting it go was not an easy matter. One thing he'd learned during his studies abroad was that each person's perception was his reality. But one's perception did not always align with truth. How one perceived a situation held far more sway over that person than the actuality of it.

Yet, he was all about truth. About seeking it. Finding it.

Living it.

And whenever truth was challenged——. Well, he had a hard time with that.

Shortly after Kofi had died in the boating accident, Jeb had finally found the real Truth in Jesus Christ. Since that day, Jeb had done his best to make all of his decisions based on Him. Yet, today, Jeb's decision against prejudice—a decision based on truth—was being challenged by the very men who knew him well, who had watched him grow up, who knew and respected his father. But, instead of aligning themselves with truth, they had aligned themselves with a tradition based on a lie.

The lie that skin color defined a person.

Jeb took a deep breath as he drove the dirt road toward his mother's house, avoiding the many potholes along the way. He rolled down the window and breathed in the hot African air. Unlike the hot, humid climate of a Pennsylvania summer, the air of Ghana was parching, making it far more bearable.

All around him, lush cocoa fields extended for miles, their rows of low-growing plants with bright green leaves standing in brilliant contrast against the blue-canopied sky. Jeb waved as he passed the smiling field workers bringing in the mid-crop harvest. Their bright return smiles helped to lift the burden that lay heavy on his heart. This was his country. These were his people. More than anything, he wanted to serve them. To give them a better life. To teach them the principles of government and economics that would help raise them to the dignity with which God had created them.

Would God not allow him that opportunity?

As he approached his mother's house, he thought of Tori. As soon as he returned to the States, he'd ask her to marry him. He would bring her here. What would she think of his country? Would she like the people? The climate? The terrain? Would she adapt well to life in his native land? She would have few amenities compared to what she now had in America. No indoor plumbing. No supermarkets. No shops in which to buy beautiful dresses. How would she fare? He would do his best to provide her with the best he could offer her, but still, she would lack many of the things to which she was accustomed. And what of friends? Would the women of his tribe accept her and befriend her, or would they consider her an outsider and refuse to give her the time of day? The women of his tribe were usually very friendly—which made him wonder even more about what had happened to Mama—but would their minds be poisoned by their husbands, some of whom sat on the tribal council of elders?

His concern for Tori's happiness and well-being was ever at the forefront of his mind, encouraging him on the one hand, terrifying him on the other. He would never forgive himself if their marriage brought her unhappiness of any kind.

That is, if she still wanted him.

After a few moments, he reached his mother's house. He found her in the kitchen, preparing the midday meal.

"Hello, Mama."

"Hello, my son."

She'd referred to him as her son. And the tone of her voice had changed. Was she softening toward him? "How was your meeting with the elders?"

"It did not go well."

She turned toward him. "And how is that?"

"They questioned my character." He took in a deep breath. "Kofi's father accused me of the crime of killing his son."

Mama's eyes teared. "But, why?"

"I think he has never forgiven me for the accident."

Mama sat down at the kitchen table, her lips trembling. "And now he is trying to keep you from the chieftaincy."

"Yes. But, I think that the council is more concerned that I have already chosen the woman I want to marry and that she is white." Jeb placed a palm on the table. "Would you believe they did not even question me on tribal policy? On my goals for the future of our tribe? On my plans for bringing our people out of poverty and illiteracy? No, nothing like that. I was amazed. And, frankly, angered."

Mama turned her gaze toward him. "If they do not first resolve the issue of your marriage, nothing else matters to them."

"But how narrow-minded is that?

She did not respond.

"Of course! You agree with them. You've made it clear that you agree with them." His face flushed. "You don't want me to choose my own wife, either. Like the elders, you care more about your outdated tradition and stupid prejudice than about your own son!"

Mama remained silent.

"What about loving all people as Jesus taught? And as you yourself taught me? What happened to your Christian faith, Mama? You are not acting according to what the Lord requires of us."

A guilty look crossed Mama's face, but still she remained silent.

Bile rose to Jeb's throat. He'd had enough. "I'm leaving this afternoon to go back to America. I don't care what the elders decide. If they want me, they know where to find me. But, I will tell you—and I will tell them—that I will not accept the chieftaincy unless the tribe accepts my wife! My decision is firm and final!"

He stormed from the room. He would pack his bags and catch the next plane from Accra to the States. He had only one goal: to get back to Tori as soon as possible. She alone was his love. His future.

His life.

And if marrying her meant giving up the chieftaincy, so be it!

Chapter 8

It was late afternoon by the time Tori left the University of Pennsylvania Police Department where she'd reported the assault. After her difficult conversation with Pop, she'd conceded to notifying the police despite the assailant's threats. The more people knew about the incident, the better. Exposure might make the assailant think twice before carrying out his threats to harm her.

The late-December day was frigid and damp, sending chills through Tori's already cold bones. She pulled her knit hat down over her ears, more to hide her face than to keep warm. She didn't want to risk the assailant's recognition should she run into him.

The university police had required her to fill out and sign several forms. They would notify the Philadelphia police, they explained, and both divisions would work together investigating the case. Meanwhile, Tori would need to be vigilant.

Still shaking from having to relive the event while filing the report, she walked across campus to the bus stop for her trip home. Every few steps, she looked over her shoulder to see if anyone was following her. She'd never been one to be paranoid, but today she was.

Today, she also missed Jeb more than ever. He'd been gone almost a week. Did he think of her as much as she thought of him? Did he miss her as much as she missed him? Had he told his family and the tribal elders about her?

Tori usually considered herself a patient person, but the word *patient* was not in her vocabulary today. She needed to know where she stood with Jeb. Would he return to her—for her? Or would seeing the rich, dark beauty of the women of his tribe cause him to forget her? Would the tribe's choice of a wife for him sweep Jeb off his feet? Surely the elders would choose the most beautiful woman among them. The most intelligent. The most alluring.

Tori shuddered at the thought. Did absence really make the heart grow fonder? Or was the truth, *Out of sight, out of mind?* If her experience were any indication, now that she was out of Jeb's sight, she would be more on his mind than ever, wouldn't she?

A blast of winter wind whipped around her neck, sending a shiver down her back. She plodded onward, pushing against the rising wind toward the bus stop a block away. Because of the darkening skies, streetlights had turned on earlier than usual.

The weather forecast called for several inches of snow. Already, a few flakes had started to fall and covered the sidewalk with a thin blanket of white marked by the footprints of passersby hurrying to their destinations. The occasional honking of a car horn punctuated the sound of city traffic.

Tori reached the bus stop just as the lumbering bus pulled up to the curb and filled the air with diesel fumes, its brakes hissing to a full stop. Clutching her purse to her side, she climbed aboard and found a seat in the last row. She felt safe there. No one could take her by surprise.

The bus at this time of day was almost filled to capacity. It pulled away from the curb like a ship pulling away from its moorings. Slowly. Carefully. Deliberately.

Tori gazed out the window. The snow fell more heavily now, in large, plump flakes that promised several inches before nightfall. By the time she exited the bus, a thick layer of white had blanketed the ground. She hurried along the block between the bus stop and her home. She waved to her neighbor returning from work, a metal lunch pail tucked under his arm.

As Tori entered the house, Anna's voice greeted her from the kitchen. "You got a telegram from Ghana!"

Her heart pounding, Tori quickly removed her coat and gloves and headed toward the kitchen.

Anna grinned and handed her the envelope. "Western Union delivered it only a few moments ago." She smiled knowingly. "I think it's from Jeb."

Tori's heart pounded as her fingers nervously tore open the telegram. Her gaze flew over the words. *Leaving Accra tonight. Will arrive in Philadelphia tomorrow evening. Miss you terribly. Jeb.*

Tori's heart skipped a beat. Tomorrow evening? So soon? So the elders had allowed Jeb to return to the States to complete his studies? What about the chieftaincy?

So many questions bombarded her mind. But overshadowing them all were the words *Miss you terribly.*

Jeb missed her! Not only missed her, but missed her *terribly.*

Her heart locked onto that word as a magnet locks onto iron. Jeb didn't reject her. He really missed her.

Could it be possible that he even loved her?

She could hardly contain herself. Soon she would be reunited with the man she loved. Nothing else mattered. Not the assault. Not the racism. Not Pop's objections. Nothing! All that mattered was that Jeb missed her and was coming home.

Tori turned toward her sister, who had been patiently waiting while Tori read the telegram. "Anna! Jeb will be home tomorrow night!" Excitement lit her voice.

"That was a quick trip."

"Yes." Tori grew pensive. "Its brevity could be interpreted in two ways: Either Jeb was accepted as chief and allowed to finish his studies, or he was rejected as chief."

Anna placed a hand on Tori's arm. "What do you think will happen next?"

"I don't know. All that I know is Jeb is on his way home." Tears welling up in her eyes, Tori looked at Anna. "And that's enough for me."

* * * *

The airplane rumbled across the Atlantic Ocean, rocking Jeb into a fitful sleep. He'd left Ghana abruptly, with an uncomfortable farewell to his mother and brother. Both had been offended by his decision to marry Tori without the permission of the tribe. Both had made it clear that they would not welcome a white woman as a member of their family nor as the wife of their chief.

Both had deeply pierced his heart.

Jeb shifted in his seat, trying to find the best position for rest. But no rest came. Neither for his body, nor for his soul. The deep disappointment of his recent interview with the tribal elders weighed heavily upon him. It was one thing to be questioned for his ability, but quite another to be questioned for his character. All of his life, he'd worked hard at being a person of impeccable integrity. He'd labored to earn and maintain the trust of his family and his tribe. To see both now question his loyalty was a hard pill to swallow.

Jeb knew that the main issue at play was not Kofi's tragic death. Although that was presented as a reason, it was really an excuse. Not once over the intervening years had the elders, nor anyone else in the tribe, accused him of responsibility for his friend's death. Immediately after the incident, the tribe had exhibited great understanding and compassion in the midst of Jeb's grief. Even Kofi's father and mother had forgiven him. At least, they'd said so.

No. Something more was going on.

Apartheid. His people simply did not want their chief to marry a white woman.

He glanced at his wristwatch. By now, the elders had convened and reached a decision regarding the chieftaincy. His failure to appear before them as instructed would have given them even more reason to reject him. But Jeb would not play their games. He would not bow to their hypocrisy.

To their racism.

The chieftaincy was rightfully his by birth. If the elders denied it to him, it would be on their heads.

Jeb directed his thoughts to the future.

Tori should have received his telegram by now. By the time he reached Philadelphia, she would have just reported for duty at the restaurant. She often worked on Tuesdays. He'd take a chance that he would find her there.

He leaned his head on the headrest and smiled as he pictured the look on Tori's face when he walked in the door. That beautiful face that had eternally engraved itself on his heart. Her honey-colored hair. Her bright hazel eyes, as soft as the sands of the Gold Coast. The delightful dimple in her cheek that accented her beautiful smile.

Thinking of her made him realize all the more how much he loved her. If he timed his arrival well, he'd get to the restaurant just as Tori started her evening shift. He'd make arrangements to come back and pick her up when she finished, and then he'd take her to their favorite café where he'd tell her all that had happened to him in Ghana and catch up on what had happened in her life while he was gone.

The stewardess stood in the aisle and made an announcement. "Ladies and gentlemen, we will be landing in thirty minutes. Please gather your belongings."

Jeb's heart leapt. Soon, the plane would land in New York. There, he would board another flight to Philadelphia where he would once again be reunited with his beloved.

* * * *

Tori stepped off the bus onto the brick sidewalk that led to *Le Garçon Bleu*, the upscale French restaurant in Old City where she worked as a hostess. A cold winter breeze whipped her face, making her eyes water. In the distance, barely visible through the tall buildings that blocked its view, an orange-russet sky lined the horizon.

Tori loved Old City, the historic part of Philadelphia's Center City downtown, with its brownstone houses, cobblestone streets, and brick sidewalks dating back more than two centuries. Although her father had come from Italy to America as an infant, her emotional roots lay deep in this area of her birth. If she married Jeb, she might have to leave it. The thought of doing so triggered a pang of nostalgia in her soul.

She quickened her pace, not wanting to be late for work. She arrived just as the early crowd started to dribble in. Wealthy widows, prominent businessmen, famous actors, actresses, artists, and musicians—all frequented this topnotch restaurant in Old City. She'd gotten to rub shoulders with many of them and remained no more impressed than before.

Tori swung open the heavy oaken door and entered. Bill Randolph, her boss and owner of the restaurant, stood at the reception podium, reviewing the evening's menu.

"Hello, Mr. Randolph." Tori interrupted him.

"Hello, Tori. You look happy tonight." Bill greeted her with a smile.

"I am." She grinned from ear to ear. "My boyfriend returns tonight."

Mr. Randolph looked up. "Oh. Returns from where?"

"From Ghana."

"Did he go there on business?"

"No. He's a native of Ghana."

Mr. Randolph gave her a disapproving look. "I see. Is he black?"

Tori's muscles tensed. "Yes. Why do you ask?"

"Just curious."

The look on Mr. Randolph's face troubled Tori.

"Please make sure he doesn't stop by to visit you here."

"Oh, don't worry. He won't. He's much too polite and respectful for that. He would never interfere with my duties toward you and our clients." She hesitated, a disturbing thought niggling at the back of her mind. "But would it matter if he stops by during my break?"

Mr. Randolph cleared his throat. "Tori, as you know, we have a sophisticated clientèle here. I wouldn't want to do anything that could jeopardize business."

An alarm sounded in Tori's heart. "What do you mean?"

"I mean that some white folks—well—let's just say that some white folks don't see eye-to-eye with black folks."

She looked at him askance, understanding dawning in her mind. "Mr. Randolph, are you insinuating that my black boyfriend is inferior to a white man?"

Mr. Randolph hesitated, lowered his eyes, and then raised them again. "Let me just say that some of our white clients would not appreciate eating in the same restaurant with a black man present."

Tori clenched her fists. First the assault on campus, and now this. "To my knowledge, Mr. Randolph, there is no law on the books in Pennsylvania—nor here in the northern United States, for that matter—that forbids a black man from entering or eating in a restaurant with white people."

Mr. Randolph protested. "A law doesn't have to be on the books for public sentiment to enforce it. If you've noticed, we don't have black people frequenting this restaurant."

She had never noticed, oblivious as she was to skin color. But now that Mr. Randolph mentioned it, she'd never seen a black person eat at her restaurant. How strange! Was there some unspoken law she didn't know about? Had word spread among the Negro community that black people were unwelcome here? Why hadn't a black person challenged that unspoken law?

Mr. Randolph released a long breath. "Philadelphia is a big small town. We insiders know exactly what's going on. If you want to keep your job, you'll tell your boyfriend to stay away. Understood?"

Bile rose to Tori's throat. No, she didn't understand, and never would. Nor would she continue working in a place that espoused racism.

Her blood boiled. "Frankly, Mr. Randolph, I am shocked and incensed at your comment. I will *not* tell my boyfriend to stay away from the restaurant on the grounds of his skin color. This is a free country. At least, I thought it was up until now. My boyfriend is not a criminal. He is a fine man. A far better man than you, in fact." She glared at him. "And before you fire me, I quit!"

Mr. Randolph leaned toward her and whispered. "Would you kindly keep your voice down? You are drawing the attention of our clients and disrupting their eating pleasure."

It took everything within Tori to keep from slapping his face.

At that instant, Jeb walked into the restaurant, wearing a broad grin.

Tori's jaw dropped. "Jeb!" She rushed into his arms and embraced him.

"I just had to stop by to see you before going to my apartment."

Instantly, Mr. Randolph stood beside them. "I'm afraid you will have to leave the premises. You are making a scene." He directed his comment to Jeb.

Every fiber in Tori's body stretched close to snapping point. "Very well, Mr. Randolph. We're leaving."

"Not you, Tori. You're on duty tonight."

"Sorry, but I told you I quit." She grabbed her purse. "And I assure you, Mr. Randolph, that this is not the end of the matter. You're not dealing with a couple of wimps here." She drew in a deep breath and raised her chin. "You're dealing with royalty!"

Still holding her chin high, she took Jeb's arm and smiled at him. "It's time to go, Jeb. To move onward to bigger and better things."

Jeb nodded, and, placing his warm hand over hers, they left the restaurant.

Once outside, Tori took a deep breath of the cold, evening air.

Never, in all of her life, had she felt more like a queen.

Chapter 9

Seated at a small, secluded back table at their favorite campus café, Jeb and Tori talked into the late hours of the night. He recounted to her all the events of his short stay in Ghana. His refusal to comply with the elders' choice of a wife for him. His mother's objection to his marrying a white woman. His difficult interview before the council of elders and the matter of Kofi's death and Jeb's assumed cowardice. One by one, Jeb poured out his heart to Tori while she listened with all of hers.

The joy of being with her again dispelled the pain of all the obstacles that had come against him during his stay in Ghana. Her presence made them all pale in comparison to being with her once again. To basking in her beauty.

To reveling in the loveliness of her character.

He could not imagine a future without her.

Jeb leaned toward Tori and took her hand in his. He drew in a deep breath. "Tori, I need to ask your forgiveness. I've been so foolish. When we parted at the airport, I was in a painful emotional state. I was grieving over my father, worried about the chieftaincy, and, truthfully, worried about you. I was afraid to express my true feelings for you because I didn't know what God wanted for me. For us. I needed to know His will. I prayed a lot while I was away. Now I know what God wants, and I want it, also."

Tori bit her lip.

Jeb continued. "I'm convinced He wants us together, and I will fight to make that happen."

Tears streamed down Tori's face. "Oh, Jeb! I forgive you." Her gaze was locked on his. "I, too, have thought about us a lot since our meeting at the airport. Frankly, I left there a total mess. Angry. Confused. Feeling betrayed. But after calming down and praying, I put our relationship in God's hands. Now, I, too, feel that we're meant to be together. And I'll also fight for us. No matter what."

Jeb's heart filled with courage. "I've made a decision. Unless the elders choose to accept me as their chief, I will not return to Ghana but will remain in the States. But if they do choose to accept me as their chief, I will feel obliged to assume the position, since it would be my duty by inheritance to do so."

"Indeed, it would. When will you know of their decision?"

"They were to make it last night, so I will know shortly. I instructed my mother to have the chief elder send me a telegram."

Tori nodded. "May God's will prevail."

"Yes. Only God's will. That's all I desire." Jeb gently stroked the top of her hand.

"Jeb, whatever happens, I want you to know that I support you all the way."

"That means everything to me." He raised her hand and kissed it tenderly. "Now that I've unburdened my heart to you, tell me about what has been going on with you while I was away."

Tori proceeded to tell Jeb about Susanna's alarming warning in the library, about Tori's subsequent assault on campus, and about the assailant's threat to her.

Jeb's face grew dark. "Had I been here, I would have destroyed the man."

"I'm glad you weren't here. You are a foreigner. You could have gotten yourself into a lot of trouble." She chuckled. "A most unbecoming thing for a chief."

He locked his gaze onto hers. "I would give my life to protect you."

A sublime look crossed her face. Jeb realized he'd touched a deep chord within her.

Tori also told Jeb about her father's angry reaction upon learning that she was dating a black man, and about her boss's hateful warning just prior to Jeb's arrival at the restaurant.

Jeb sighed. "It is getting really ugly." His muscles tensed. "I thought that racism was bad in Ghana, but I see it is almost as bad here in America." His heart quickened as he looked deep into her eyes. "It is wrong of me to put you through all of this."

"You are doing nothing wrong, Jeb. The wrong lies in the people who espouse racism. The problem lies within their hearts. They have chosen to believe a lie and to live according to that lie."

"Yes, but look at how their behavior is affecting you. Until you met me, you were happy and free of such troubles." He looked around at the other customers in the café. "Even now as we sit here, watchful eyes are upon us. Judging us. Whispering lies about us. Condemning us."

She smiled. "Then we will simply have to be more vigilant. That's all."

Jeb nodded in agreement. "Much more vigilant. Those we deem our friends may actually be our enemies." He thought of Yafeu and the tribal elders, and his heart panged.

"True. But does it really matter what people think about us?"

"No. What people think about us doesn't matter. But what does matter is how their thinking will adversely affect us. Because it will, Tori. It will."

Tori nodded, a pensive look on her face.

Jeb hesitated. "If you continue in a relationship with me, there will be much suffering. There will be racism. Rejection. Alienation. Isolation. Misunderstanding. There will be threats.

Verbal abuse. Maybe even physical abuse. There will be the pain of watching our children suffer because they do not fit in. There will be pressure to compromise. To give in. To give up the fight." He squeezed her hand. "This will be your lot in life, dear one. Are you willing to embrace it?"

Jeb realized his words were nothing short of a marriage proposal. Yet, he had to speak them. For many days now, he'd wanted to ask Tori to marry him. But he loved her too much not to warn her of the kind of life she would have if she *did* marry him. He wanted to be sure she fully understood the ramifications of marrying a black man—and a possible tribal chief at that. He'd lived in apartheid Africa too long not to know the evil that racism truly was and the abject darkness that it brought.

Tori's eyes moistened. "Jeb, don't you think I have not pondered those questions over and over again myself? What I experienced while you were away showed me the dark side of humanity. A side I had only heard of but now have seen with my very own eyes. And, yes, it is ugly. Uglier than I had imagined." She gripped his hand more tightly. "But the Bible says that love never fails. That means Love. Never. Fails." She repeated the words slowly, emphasizing each one.

A lump formed in Jeb's throat. He wanted to take her into his arms and never let her go. "Tori Pendola, you are the most amazing woman I have ever met!"

The glow on her face warmed his heart. Soon he would formally ask her to marry him. At their favorite spot down by the river. He pictured it in his mind's eye. There, on their special bench by the riverside, he would ask Tori Pendola to be his wife. There, he would pledge his love to her for all the remaining days of their lives.

In spite of what those remaining days might bring.

* * * *

That night, after spending several hours with Jeb at the *Penn-Ultimate Café*, Tori lay in bed, reliving the events of the evening. Jeb's questions to her as they opened up their hearts to each other played over and over again in her mind, giving her no rest. Would she, indeed, be able to handle the pressures that would inevitably come with a black-and-white relationship and that would come even more fiercely with a black-and-white marriage? Would she be able to withstand the debasing words against her and Jeb and, later, against their children?

While Jeb asked her the hard questions, she'd read his heart. He was really asking her if she loved him enough to marry him in the face of the suffering that prejudice always brought. She'd already asked herself that same question. Dozens of times. And she'd already answered it as well. Yes! She loved Jeb enough to face and overcome every single obstacle that would come against them, no matter what.

Where would the prejudice show up next? And in what way?

Would it ever end?

She turned onto her side and faced the window. A full moon shone brightly through the open curtains, lighting up the night sky and casting long, white beams across her bed before cascading onto the hardwood floor. She gazed at the moon. It shone over blacks and whites, without discrimination, giving equal light to everyone. She pondered the irony of it all. The moon had more sense than some people.

Tori sighed. Until meeting Jeb, she'd never experienced the bitter racist war personally. She'd always been a spectator to the ugly drama, never an actor in it. Sure, as she was growing up, her father had often expressed an intense dislike of black people. *Colored,* he called them. Complaining that their inroads into white neighborhoods decreased property values, introduced crime, and, worst of all, invited interracial marriage.

She cringed. What would Pop do if he knew that she and Jeb were contemplating marriage?

He would disown her for sure.

Tori shuddered. Rejection had never been easy for her.

The bedroom door creaked open as Anna entered. "So, here you are. I was looking for you. I want to hear all about what happened."

Tori had informed Anna—and only Anna—of Jeb's arrival that evening.

"So, how did things go?"

"Great with Jeb and me. Not so great otherwise."

"Tough day?"

"More than tough."

Anna dropped onto her bed and crisscrossed her legs. "Tell me about it."

Tori proceeded to tell Anna about the racial prejudice she and Jeb had encountered that evening at the restaurant. "It was horrible, Anna. Mr. Randolph had the gall to humiliate Jeb in front of the clientèle."

Anna listened intently, surprise and then disgust registering in her clear brown eyes. "So, what did you do?"

"I gave Mr. Randolph a piece of my mind, and then I quit."

"Good for you! Seems to me that something should be done to stop this craziness."

"I guess we could post a complaint, but what would that accomplish? Besides, Jeb is a foreigner. As far as I can tell, he may have no legal recourse in this country."

"I hear you."

"If they only knew that in his country he is royalty." Tori sat up and drew her knees to her chest.

Anna chuckled. "Indeed!"

"Anna, I think Jeb is going to ask me to marry him."

"Really?" Anna was all smiles. "What makes you say that?"

"He asked me some very serious questions about the challenges we would face as a black and white couple in a racist world." Tori looked at her sister. "I've already experienced some of those challenges firsthand, like the assault." She sighed. "But who knows what worse challenges may lie ahead."

"No one knows, Tori. But that should not be your deciding factor. It seems to me that you have to ask yourself only one question: Do you love Jeb enough to face those challenges?"

Without hesitation, Tori responded. "Oh, yes, Anna! I have no doubt that I love him enough."

"Then, as I see it, that's your answer."

Tori laughed. Anna was ever the practical one.

"No matter what decision we make, there's always a set of consequences to that decision. So, bottom line, we have to make the decision that aligns with God's will for our lives."

Anna was right.

In the depths of her heart, Tori knew she'd made the right decision.

* * * *

Nearly two months had transpired and Jeb still had not heard from chief elder Siisi Odamtten. Were the elders still deliberating about his chieftaincy? It seemed impossible. He'd expected they'd have a decision within a day—or much sooner than now.

Something must have happened.

But no news was good news.

Or so he hoped. If he didn't hear anything by the end of the week, he would send a telegram to the chief elder.

At 8:30 a.m., Jeb hurried to his World Economics class. February was about to close its doors. A light breeze filled the air, bringing with it thoughts of an early spring. A few weeks earlier, Punxsutawney Phil, the famous groundhog, had not seen his shadow, indicating the soon end of winter. While Jeb took the groundhog's prediction with a grain of salt, it was pleasant to know that spring would soon displace winter.

When Jeb reached his classroom, most of the students were already seated and waiting for their consistently late professor. Jeb took his usual seat at the end of the second row and settled in. Light chatter filled the room as the students complained of their professor's perpetual tardiness. Some threatened to leave, while others invoked the ten-minute rule that allowed a professor a ten-minute grace period before students could leave without repercussion.

Jeb opened his book to review the day's assignment.

"So, you're dating one of our women, are you?"

The derogatory comment from a male student to his left startled him. His muscles tensing, Jeb turned toward the student. "What do you mean?"

"You know very well what I mean. You're dating one of our white women." He emphasized the word *white*.

Jeb's blood ran hot. "Why do you ask?"

"I saw you together at the campus café last night. You seemed to be having a good time."

The *Penn-Ultimate Café* had become Jeb and Tori's favorite meeting place. Nearly every night they met there to catch up on the day, to talk about their future, and just to be together.

Jeb hadn't noticed anyone else in the café the night before. His eyes had been focused only and entirely on Tori.

Drawing on all of his polite upbringing, Jeb searched for the right words to reply. "Yes, we do enjoy each other's company."

The student leaned over toward Jeb and spoke in low tones. "I suggest you stop enjoying each other's company." He gave Jeb a hard stare. "And sooner rather than later."

Jeb clenched his jaw. "Excuse me, but what right do you have to suggest such a thing?"

The young man's eyes narrowed. "Look, black man, you're a foreigner. You have no rights here, you understand? If it were up to us whites, we'd ship you back to your own country in an instant. We don't want colored people invading our territory."

The words stung.

Just as Jeb formulated a response, the professor entered the classroom, interrupting the conversation.

The next hour passed by in a blur as Jeb struggled to cope with his worst personal experience of prejudice since coming to America. An experience that he hadn't expected and that he didn't like one bit. Surely a university campus, a bastion for free and open discourse among equals, should be the last place to find racial prejudice.

Yet, the undercurrent of racism remained strong, even here in the North. Blacks sensed it more than whites, perhaps because blacks, more than whites, were the victims of racism.

As the class came to an end, Jeb gathered his books and then turned to confront the racist student to give him a piece of his mind. But the young man had already disappeared. Perhaps a blessing in disguise, to keep Jeb from losing his patience and embarrassing himself.

And from getting into big trouble.

His heart heavy, Jeb left the classroom and headed for the library to work on his thesis. Deep in thought, he walked across the lawn that led from the classroom building to the library. The air was fresh and clean with the sweet fragrance of winter pine. It was a beautiful day for a stroll along the river with Tori.

On impulse, he decided to walk over to the art building. Her nine o'clock class would have just ended, so maybe he'd find her there.

Jeb arrived just as Tori left the lecture hall. Fearing she would not see him, he called to her.

At the sound of her name, she turned and burst into a bright smile. Her eyes went wide with delight. "Jeb! What are you doing here?" She eagerly approached him and took his arm.

"White slut!" The ugly slur slipped from the lips of a student passing behind Jeb.

Jeb winced, hoping Tori hadn't heard it.

The pained look on her face told him she had.

"I'm so sorry, Tori."

She braved a smile. "No need to apologize for someone else's stupidity."

Jeb could tell she was reeling from the wicked comment but wouldn't let it knock her down. He took a deep breath. "I was headed to the library and thought it too beautiful a day not to take a walk with you. Are you free?"

She smiled. "Actually, yes. I don't have another class for an hour. I'd love to take a walk with you."

"Shall we go down by the river?"

"Wonderful idea!" Shifting her books to her left arm, she slipped her right hand into his.

He squeezed it gently, longing to soothe the hurt from the uncalled-for verbal abuse. He looked at her. A light morning breeze lifted wisps of hair around Tori's lovely face. A lump formed in his throat. She was beautiful. So breathtakingly beautiful!

For a long while, they walked silently, hand in hand, as the rhythm of their hearts blended into one. Finally, Jeb spoke. "I have something to tell you."

"Yes?"

He stopped in front of a bench and turned toward her. The morning sunlight danced across her hair. He wanted so much to slip his fingers through it and caress it. But it wasn't yet time. "Let's sit down."

They sat on their favorite wooden bench, and he proceeded to recount the incident that had occurred in his economics class that morning.

Her gaze locked onto his. "I'm so sorry you had to endure that."

Jeb put his arm around her.

As he drew her close, a man's voice yelled from behind him. "Hey, boy! You're off limits with that white woman!"

Jeb felt Tori stiffen in his embrace. Then, just as quickly as she had stiffened, she relaxed and pressed even more closely into his chest.

Chapter 10

"How was your day?" Anna smiled as Tori entered their bedroom.

A soft glow came from the double-shaded turquoise lamp on the nightstand that stood between their twin beds. A small Westclox Baby Ben alarm clock stood in front of the lamp. At half-past nine, Anna was already settled in for the night, curlers on her head and a book in her hands.

"My day was ugly!" Tori dropped onto her bed, not only physically exhausted but emotionally exhausted as well. "Uglier than ever." She lay down on her back, her head on her pillow and her hands folded on her stomach. Her aching muscles were no match for the ache in her heart at the injustices she and Jeb had experienced that day.

"What happened?" Anna put down the novel she was reading.

"Jeb got threatened by a white guy in his class for dating me. The guy warned him to stop dating a white girl. Said that white girls belonged to white guys and were off limits to blacks."

Anna drew her knees up to her chest and leaned forward.

"Then, when Jeb caught up with me later on campus, someone called me a slut."

Anna sat up straight. "What a horrible thing to say!" Compassion edged her voice. "I'm so sorry, Tori."

"Thanks. I can't believe how rude people can be."

"'Rude' is putting it mildly." A worried look crossed Anna's face. "Be careful, Tori. These people will do anything to get their point across. Just think of the horror going on in Africa with apartheid."

"But we're not in Africa! We're in America!"

"Don't think for one minute that the same sentiments don't exist here. Whites and blacks can't even marry in some states."

Tori grabbed the battered teddy bear that had been her refuge since her first birthday and had sat on her bed ever since. "I refuse to give in to this ugliness, Anna. So far just today, between the two of us, Jeb and I have experienced three episodes of racism. But we're going to continue dating no matter what anyone says or does. This is a free country." She hesitated. "Or so I thought."

"Yes, that's true. But there are a lot of crazy people out there who don't think the same way you do. In fact, they think the exact opposite." Anna tilted her head. "Like Pop."

Tori's stomach roiled. "Anna, I'm in love with Jeb. And nothing is going to keep me from having a relationship with him."

"I didn't suggest you should break off the relationship. Just be careful."

Anna's words brought a chill to Tori's veins. She tried to lighten the danger. "Maybe I'll hire you as my bodyguard."

Anna laughed. "Well, I can kick and scream and make a frightening face, but I don't think that will help much." Anna grew pensive. "Seriously, though, Tori, please be careful. I don't want you to get hurt."

"I don't want to get hurt, either." Tori studied the swirls in the plaster ceiling. They reminded her of the emotional swirling going on in her own life. "You know, I'm beginning to realize more and more that the way one thinks greatly affects one's life for either good or bad."

"How so?"

"Well, take Jeb and me, for instance. We have no problem with skin color. We don't think that blacks are inferior to whites or that whites are inferior to blacks. We think that all people are equal because all people were created equal by God. Because of the way we think, Jeb and I don't have a problem with each other, so we can enjoy a great relationship. We didn't allow skin color to keep us from developing a friendship. But if I thought otherwise—if I were a racist and thought that blacks were inferior to whites—I would never have come to know what a wonderful man Jeb is."

"Nor would he have come to know what a wonderful woman you are."

Tori's heart warmed. She turned her head toward her sister. "Thank you, Anna. You're such an encourager." Tori sighed. "I just wish Pop felt the same way about Jeb and me."

"Pop doesn't yet see the light. He's wrapped up in his own false perspective." Anna uncrossed her legs. "That's exactly what racism is. It's a false perspective. A lie."

Tori nodded.

Anna sat back against her pillow. "The problem lies on the heart level, not the physical level. Remember that verse we memorized as kids in Sunday school? 'As a man thinks in his heart, so is he'?"

Tori chuckled. "How could I forget it? Miss Ritter drilled that verse into our heads over and over again for weeks."

Anna smiled. "Well, that verse applies perfectly here. The racial issue is a direct result of how people think in their hearts about blacks and whites. Until they change their thinking, there will always be hatred between blacks and whites."

Tori sobered. "So, the real challenge is to change people's thinking."

"You got that right." Anna paused. "And only God can do that."

"But only if people want Him to."

Anna sighed. "The problem is, most people don't."

* * * *

After sending a telegram to chief elder Odamtten, Jeb left the Western Union office and walked the few blocks to his classroom building. The sounds of the city around him—the honking horns; the vendors hawking their coffee, doughnuts, and bagels; the rumbling buses—filled the morning atmosphere with life. On a street corner, a young boy pitched the morning edition of *The Philadelphia Inquirer* to passersby eager to get the latest baseball scores or updates on President Eisenhower's recently organized space race against Russia.

The late-February day was rainy and gray, with a light wind that was enough to chill Jeb's bones. He huddled under his umbrella, briefcase in hand, as rain splattered against his trousers and shoes. One thing he would not miss about the United States was the weather.

He pondered again why no word had come from the tribe nor from his mother, regarding the elders' vote on his chieftaincy. Was no news good news? Or did no news mean they had severed all ties with him? Even so, the chief elder should have notified him about the tribe's decision. A chief must at least know whether or not he will rule. He hoped he would get a reply to his telegram inquiry. Unless …

Alarm shot through Jeb's soul. Perhaps something dreadful had happened. Perhaps members of the apartheid movement had gotten word that Jeb was planning to marry a white woman and had razed his village in retaliation, killing all of his people. Such a thing would not be unheard of in apartheid Africa.

He dismissed the horrific thought. If that had happened, surely he would have heard about it in the news. Instead, he chose to focus his mind on positive thoughts. Thoughts that would uplift him.

Like thoughts of Tori.

Tonight he would propose to her. He had it all planned out. He would take her to a Baroque concert at the Academy of Music, followed by dinner at *Giovanni's Ristorante*, a romantic Italian restaurant in Center City that Tori loved. After dinner, they'd take a cab to their favorite spot along the Schuylkill River, where he would ask Tori to marry him.

Anticipation filled Jeb's heart as he looked forward to their evening together and to a lifetime with the woman he loved.

He crossed the street and headed for the economics building. A twinge of panic struck him. What if Tori refused his marriage proposal? Until now, he hadn't even considered that possibility. She'd already told him she loved him. Yet, with the recent incidents of prejudice—three in a single day—had her resolve weakened? She'd promised him at the time that it hadn't. But what about later, after she'd really had a chance to consider the implications? Had the ugly, firsthand experiences shaken her and awakened her to the truth that their life together would be far from easy? That it would, indeed, be far more difficult than the life of a white couple or a Negro couple?

Jeb tried unsuccessfully to calm his nerves. The only thing he could do was to wait until tonight for Tori's response.

He reached his classroom just as class started. The professor gave him a perfunctory nod as Jeb slipped into an empty seat in the back. He scanned the room for the student who had insulted him the day before and found him in the second row.

Jeb tensed. As much as he was tempted to give the student a piece of his mind, the better part of valor would be to ignore the insult and forgive him. To stoop to the student's level would be to disgrace himself. Jeb would let God defend and vindicate him.

After classes that day, he called the restaurant to confirm the reservation and then double-checked his wallet to make sure he had the concert tickets. All was ready.

Especially his heart.

Looking back, he realized he'd fallen in love with Tori the first night he'd met her at the museum lecture four months earlier. Since then, his love for her had only grown, to the point that he wanted to spend the rest of his life with her. Yet, many challenges still lay ahead, among which were the most difficult ones involving Tori's parents, his family, and his tribe. All of them were vehemently opposed to their marriage. All of them would require handling with kid gloves. But he and Tori would prevail through their love and the power of God within them.

Jeb hurried back to his dorm to get ready for the big evening. When he arrived, he found Kelechi poring over his books.

Kelechi looked up. "Hey, man! Where have you been?"

"In class. I had a full load today. My head is spinning."

Kelechi laughed. "Your head has been spinning since you met Tori."

Jeb sat down at the table across from his roommate. "Guess what?"

"What?"

"I'm going to propose to her tonight."

Kelechi slapped his hand on the table. "Well, it's about time! What's been holding you back?"

"Perhaps my very love for her."

"What do you mean?"

"I've been so concerned about the severe prejudice she will face if we marry. She's already experienced an assault and some ugly verbal abuse. Thank God she hasn't experienced the violence we've seen in Africa." Jeb sighed. "I'm concerned, Kelechi. I don't want her to be unhappy and in danger for the rest of her life."

Kelechi leaned forward. "Jeb, listen to me. If Tori loves you, none of this stuff will matter to her." He smiled. "Have you never heard the expression, 'Love conquers all'?"

Kelechi was right. Jeb already knew that truth. If Tori truly loved him, nothing else would matter. Not prejudice, nor insults, nor rejection. True love never failed. And their love was true. It would hold them together and enable them to overcome every obstacle. It would take them through the fire of hatred and oppression. Through the deep waters of misunderstanding and fear.

"Yes, you're right. I have to keep that truth in mind and focus on it."

Kelechi leaned back in his chair. "So, my friend, where are you going to propose?"

"By the river, where we often walk. But first, I'm going to take her to dinner at *Giovanni's Ristorante* and then to a concert at the Academy of Music."

"Wow! You've become quite the high roller, haven't you?"

Jeb laughed heartily. "Tori is absolutely worth it. Marriage is a lifelong commitment, so I might as well make the most of my proposal, right?"

"Right!"

Jeb rose. "Well, I'd better shower and dress. I have to meet Tori at six."

Kelechi rose as well and extended a hand to Jeb. "Congratulations, my friend! As we say in Nigeria, 'May you and Tori be a light for each other all the days of your lives.'"

Tears welled up in Jeb's eyes. "Thank you, Kelechi." Jeb embraced his friend. "By the way, did I tell you I want you to be best man at my wedding?"

Kelechi's eyes grew wide as they filled with tears. "You could not have given me a greater honor, my friend."

Jeb smiled. "Nor could you have given me a greater honor than by accepting."

Now Jeb needed only one thing more—the highest honor of having Tori agree to becoming his wife.

* * * *

Shortly after 5:00 p.m., Tori slipped out of the house. Only Anna knew she'd be meeting Jeb for dinner and a concert at the Academy of Music. And Anna was sworn to secrecy. Ever since her grievous encounter with her father, Tori didn't dare mention a word about Jeb.

Pop had hardly spoken with her since their fateful conversation two months earlier when she'd told him about the assault and about dating Jeb. Since then, any dialogue she and Pop had engaged in had been strained and hurtful. This morning, when he'd run into her in the hallway, he'd ignored her and hurried away. The memory still stung deeply.

Mom, while aloof, had, at least, spoken with Tori. But Mom was the type who didn't want to rock the boat. Nor did she want to cross her husband, even when she knew he was wrong.

Tori sighed. There wasn't much she could do but pray.

And find another place to live as soon as possible.

Meanwhile, she wouldn't let anything interfere with tonight's date with Jeb. She would be happy, not only for herself, but for him as well. There would be time enough later to figure out what to do about her parents.

A twinge of guilt pricked her heart. She hated hiding things from them, but their hateful and unreasonable attitude toward Jeb had made it necessary. If only they knew what a wonderful man he was. If only they realized how highly esteemed and respected he was by those who knew him.

If only they would give Jeb a chance!

But Pop had closed his mind to all reasoning. He'd allowed fear to dominate his thinking. Fear ruled by misinformation and the lies that always accompanied prejudice.

Plagued with guilt and regret, yet drawn by love, she hurried toward the bus stop to catch the Broad Street bus to the Academy of Music. The evening was cool, but not frigid. Signs of winter's end were all around. The last vestiges of snow melted on the rooftops. An orange crocus peeked through the ground along the sidewalk. An early robin, perched on the bare limb of a nearby beech tree, chirped happily.

Catching her breath, Tori arrived just as the bus pulled up to the curb and boarded it. She and Jeb had agreed to meet in a nearby restaurant before the concert. Sadly, because of Pop, Jeb was forbidden to escort her from her home as he wanted to do.

Several blocks later, the bus came to a halt at the corner near the restaurant. As Tori descended, she found Jeb waiting, a lovely bouquet of red roses in his hand.

Filled with joy, she practically leapt from the bus into his waiting arms.

Smiling broadly, he spun her around and then placed her gently on the sidewalk, handing her the bouquet of flowers.

She smiled and breathed in their fragrance. "They're lovely! Thank you! But what's the special occasion?"

His gaze penetrated her. "*You* are the occasion." His voice was husky.

Tori swallowed hard, unspeakable joy filling her soul. "They're beautiful, Jeb!" Clutching the bouquet to her chest with her right hand, she slipped her left arm through his as they walked to the restaurant.

Giovanni's Ristorante was a romantic little place, nestled between two large buildings and hardly noticeable from the street. Yet, its reputation as one of the best Italian restaurants in Philadelphia had spread far and wide along the entire East Coast.

As Tori entered, the aroma of fresh garlic and tomatoes filled her nostrils, whetting her appetite. The clatter of plates and utensils floated from the kitchen into the main dining room, while on the walls, stunning landscapes of the Amalfi coast and Mount Vesuvius welcomed them into Italy.

Giving them a questioning look, the host seated them at a table in the far corner, overlooking a courtyard whose focal point was a large, cascading fountain. Around the fountain, beds of winter aconite and dainty snowdrops graced the area, adding to the romantic atmosphere.

Tori smiled at Jeb. "This is enchanting!"

His gaze locked on hers. "Yes, you are."

Tori's face grew warm. His deep, dark eyes harbored a mystery that she longed to explore.

The waiter brought them menus. A wide variety of entrées made it difficult to choose, but Tori finally settled on the *Scaloppine di Vitello.*

She turned to Jeb. "What are you going to have?"

"I've decided on the *Vitello alla Parmigiana.*"

Tori laughed. "So you like veal, too."

"Yes." He grew serious. "Another thing we have in common."

Tori considered his words. "We have a lot in common, don't we?"

"Yes, more in common than not." His eyes locked onto hers.

She nodded. "Over the past three months we've been dating, I've discovered that."

"Yes. Yet, who would have thought we'd have anything in common. We come from opposite sides of the world. We grew up in radically different cultures. But I feel as though I've known you all of my life."

Tori smiled. Each moment with Jeb knitted her heart more inseparably to his.

The waiter returned with their meals and placed them on the table. "*Buon appetito!*" He smiled and then left.

"What does that mean?"

"It literally means 'good appetite.' Basically, he said, 'May the meal stimulate a good appetite.'"

"In other words, may the meal be good enough to whet your appetite."

Tori laughed. "Exactly!"

As she savored every bite of her food, a strolling violinist stopped by their table, playing a haunting love song made popular only a few years earlier. She instantly recognized it as "Te Voglio Bene Tanto Tanto," a Neapolitan song recorded by Renato Rascel. One of the ways Pop maintained his native ties to Italy was by keeping up with the latest hit songs. Each year, one of his Italian cousins would send him the sheet music for the best songs of that year. Pop would learn them and play them on his accordion.

Tori sang the lyrics as the violinist played. As the child of a first-generation immigrant, she'd had the privilege of learning the Italian language, a skill for which she was most grateful.

The violinist gave her a broad smile and then moved on to the next table.

Jeb asked, "What do the words mean?"

"They mean 'I love you very, very much.'"

His eyes softening, Jeb took her hand. "I love you, Tori." The tender look in his eyes spoke volumes."

Tori's heart melted. "I love you, too, Jeb."

For the next hour, they continued to share their hearts.

He glanced at his watch. "We should probably leave. The concert will be starting soon."

Tori nodded and smiled, although saddened at having to interrupt their close meeting of hearts.

Jeb paid the bill and, in a few moments, they headed to the Academy of Music, a short walk away.

Jeb took her hand as they made their way through the crowds of people on the sidewalk.

In short order, they reached the Academy. The imposing building, with its powerful Romanesque architecture, stood before her, inviting her into its majestic halls. Tori loved this place and hoped Jeb would love it, too.

As they entered the Academy's hallowed halls, strains of the tuning orchestra floated through the air.

But they were nothing compared to the strains of love for Jeb playing in Tori's heart.

Chapter 11

The exciting strains of the Philadelphia Orchestra tuning up for its performance delighted Jeb's ears as he and Tori made their way to their seats. A uniformed usher led the way up the short flight of stairs to the mezzanine section where Jeb had purchased front-row tickets right in the center.

As he helped Tori with her coat, the fragrance of her perfume caught his senses off guard. He drank in the scent. "What perfume are you wearing? It's intoxicating."

She smiled, a hint of pink on her cheeks. "Chanel No. 5. It's the latest rage in perfumes."

Jeb made a note of the name. The perfume would make a wonderful gift for Tori in the future.

They took their seats just as the conductor introduced the evening's repertoire. Tori gently placed her bouquet of flowers on her lap, its stems safely ensconced in a vial of water.

Jeb took her right hand. Her skin felt like silk. He could barely concentrate on the music as he rehearsed what he would say when he proposed to her by the river. Over and over again, he carefully framed the words in his mind. He wanted to say them just right.

The closer the orchestra came to the end of the concert, the more his heart pounded.

Finally, the performance ended. It was time to take Tori to the river for the walk that would change their lives forever.

Jeb hailed a cab in front of the Academy. "University of Pennsylvania campus, please." Once there, Jeb and Tori would take the path that led to the Schuylkill River.

Philadelphia at night bustled with excitement. People coming out of theaters and restaurants filled the sidewalks. Marquee lights blinked against the indigo sky. Horns honked as their taxi snaked expertly through crowded streets.

But the excitement outside was nothing compared to the excitement in Jeb's heart.

They soon reached the university campus. Jeb paid the driver and helped Tori out of the cab.

He took her hand and smiled at her. "The river awaits us."

She nodded, a sweet smile on her face and delight in her eyes.

Hand in hand, they strolled the familiar path that led to the place that had become their private oasis over the last three months. Their place of refuge and safety.

Their place of rest.

When they reached their favorite bench, Tori laid her bouquet gently upon one end and then sat down.

Jeb sat down next to her.

In the distance, the Philadelphia Museum of Art, in all of its Greek Revival magnificence, illuminated the night sky and stood like a majestic guardian over the waterway. Above them hovered a full moon, casting its milky luster across the river below. The smell of honeysuckle floated through the air, while a robin trilled its melody on the branch of a nearby sycamore tree.

"Jeb, this has been an absolutely lovely evening. I can't thank you enough."

"It is I who should thank you, Tori." He put his arm around her and drew her close. "If it weren't for you, there would have been no dinner and no concert. No reason for either one." He studied her perfectly arched brows, her softly rounded cheeks, and the delicate curve of her full lips. "Thank *you* for making it possible."

She raised her head and smiled at him. "What do you mean?"

He looked into her eyes, studying their sparkle and plumbing their depths. A lump formed in his throat. "You've made me so very happy, Tori."

"I feel the same way about you, Jeb."

Her grateful smile encouraged him and motivated him to proceed. "You're my reason for living. You have given me life, and I cannot imagine being without you."

He rose from the bench and dropped to a knee in front of her.

Her eyes widened. "What are you doing?" A nervous giggle escaped her.

He pulled out a little black velvet box from the inside pocket of his jacket, lifted the lid, and removed a stunning solitaire diamond ring from its white satin bed.

Tori's jaw dropped. "Jeb! I'm speechless!"

Jeb reached for her left hand and, his own hand trembling, placed the ring gently on her ring finger. Then he gazed deeply into her tear-filled eyes.

"Tori Pendola, will you give me the honor of marrying me?" His voice quivered with the inexpressible love he felt for her.

The tears in Tori's eyes overflowed and streamed down her cheeks. "Oh, Jeb! If you only knew how I have longed for you to ask me!" She took both his hands in hers. "Yes, yes, I will marry you! I want to spend the rest of my life with you."

His heart soared as he felt the squeeze of her hands against his.

She threw her arms around his neck, held him close for a long moment, and then released him.

Jeb rose and drew her up toward himself. The whole world stood still as his mind grasped the meaning of her response. Tori Pendola, the love of his life, had agreed to marry him. To spend the rest of her life with him.

To give her life to him and to place it in his sacred care.

His heart overflowed with gratitude at this great blessing God had given him. A blessing he didn't deserve.

In the soft moonlight, he lifted her chin and kissed her for the first time. Gently. Tenderly. Drinking in the sweetness of her yielding lips.

"Stinkin' white trash!"

The harsh, ugly words suddenly shattered the heavenly atmosphere of the moment.

Jeb stiffened and turned. Standing behind him was a young white man, a cigarette dangling from his lips and hatred in his dark eyes.

His blood boiling, Jeb turned fully toward the man while protecting Tori with his back. "Excuse me, but you will not speak to my fiancée in that manner." It was the first time Jeb had called Tori his fiancée, and he loved the way it felt on his tongue.

"Says who?" The man was in his face.

Jeb glared at him. "Say I."

The man drew a step closer. "And who are you? Nothin' but a filthy—."

Bile rose to Jeb's throat as every muscle in his body went into high gear. It took everything in him to keep from striking the man and knocking him to the ground. Because of his lifelong training in tribal warfare, Jeb could easily have flattened him. Instead, Jeb practiced restraint, fearing harm to Tori should a fight break out.

Inhaling a deep breath to maintain his composure, Jeb turned away—but not before the man took a fist to Jeb's face that left him bleeding profusely from his mouth. The man then fled before Jeb could restrain him.

Tori gasped in horror. "Let's get out of here. I'm taking you to the hospital."

As quickly as they could, they made their way from the river to the street where Tori hailed a cab. She entered first and shouted to the driver. "Penn Emergency Room! And please hurry!"

Pressing his handkerchief against his mouth, Jeb followed Tori into the back seat of the taxicab. In an instant, the driver was on his way.

As the cab raced toward the hospital, Jeb's eyes remained on Tori. His heart sank. So much for a romantic marriage proposal. He ached not only for himself but also for her. Would they ever find peace and acceptance on either side of the Atlantic? Or anywhere in the world, for that matter?

Hurting too much to speak, Jeb took Tori's hand and vowed silently that, whatever it took, he would do everything humanly possible to make her life safe and happy.

Even if it meant giving up his own life to do so.

* * * *

The emergency room at the University of Pennsylvania Hospital buzzed with activity. White-coated doctors, nurses, and attendants scurried up and down the hall, tending to the many patients in the examining rooms lining it. Overflow patients lay on gurneys parked along the hallway walls as they waited for a spot to open up in an examining room. Although the hour was late, the need was great.

After a long wait, Jeb was ushered into an examining room. Tori followed and sat down in a chair in the far corner of the room. The smell of antiseptics filled her nostrils, creating an unpleasant, metallic taste in her mouth. Outside, the blare of yet another ambulance arriving at the entrance only added to the tension already present within her.

She gripped the worn, wooden arms of the chair in the examining room as the doctor examined Jeb. How many worried ones had gripped those same wooden arms, battling fear as they waited for a diagnosis?

Torn between the joy of their recent engagement and the anguish of the assault that had injured Jeb, Tori studied his handsome face, now swollen and discolored. A bluish-purple hue covered his dark skin, creating a marbled mosaic that brought tears to her eyes. Her heart wrenched.

After a series of X-rays and another long wait, the doctor completed the examination. Fortunately, Jeb's injury was far less serious than it looked. In short order, the doctor cleaned up the wound and advised Jeb to apply ice to his swollen cheek. In a couple of weeks, Jeb should be back to normal.

Holding Jeb's hand, Tori left the hospital and hailed a cab. The full moon had now reached its apex and begun its descent toward dawn. In the distance, partially hidden behind the tall buildings, a ribbon of pale blue edged the horizon. Mingled with the cacophony of city traffic, the sound of a chorus of crickets floated through the air.

Tori and Jeb entered the cab. Jeb insisted that the driver take Tori home first, even though she lived farther away. How solicitous Jeb was! How concerned for her safety and well-being! She warmed at his chivalry and at his desire to protect her.

She held his hand all the way home, longing to comfort him in his pain.

"Are you feeling better?"

"Somewhat." Jeb attempted a smile. "How about you?"

"Oh, I'm fine. Just hurting for you." Tori swallowed hard. Until tonight, she hadn't realized how much she hated to see this man suffer. How she longed to ease his pain.

Jeb stroked her hand. "I am so blessed to have you in my life." Jeb leaned toward her. "Now that we're engaged, we need to plan a wedding date."

Tori looked at him and smiled. "How about tomorrow?"

Jeb laughed and then grabbed his face in pain. "Argh! I see that I will have to refrain from laughing for a while."

Tori smiled. "That will be the most difficult part of your recovery." Jeb's delightful sense of humor was one of the traits she loved most about him.

"Seriously, Tori, don't you want to take some time to plan a nice wedding?"

Tori sobered. "I don't think there will be much of a wedding, Jeb. Pop will never walk me down the aisle, and Mom most likely won't attend the wedding, either. Only Anna will come."

"I'm sorry. But consider this. Neither will my mother be at our wedding. Only Kelechi. I've already asked him to be my best man."

Tori smiled. "I'm sure he was happy about that." She hesitated. "But your mother would come if she could, no?"

Sorrow crossed Jeb's bruised face. "I'm afraid not. As far as I know, Mama has not forgiven me for choosing to marry a white woman. Apartheid still dominates my tribe's thinking."

"Oh, Jeb. I am so sorry to have put a wedge between you and your mother." Tori's heart sank at the thought that her marriage to Jeb would estrange him from his family. Yet, wasn't that exactly what would happen to her? Hadn't her parents already expressed their strong, unwavering disapproval of Jeb just because he was black? When her parents discovered that Jeb had proposed to her and that she had accepted his proposal, they would be incensed beyond belief.

"You are not creating the wedge, dearest one! It is their wrong thinking that is creating it."

Tori clung to Jeb's hand. "How sad that a beautiful love such as ours seems to bring only heartache and hatred instead of joy and good will! Something is radically wrong."

"Yet, it is, Tori. But the wrong is not on our part. It's on the part of those who do not accept that all people have equal worth."

She nodded. "Like Pop." She'd tried to keep Pop's ultimatum from Jeb, so as not to hurt him. "He's ordered me to find my own place to live. When I told him I was dating you, he exploded. Since then, I've been searching for an apartment but haven't found one within my budget."

Jeb's eyes filled with pain. "It's because I'm black, right?"

Tori squared her jaw. "No." Her voice was firm. "It's because Pop is prejudiced."

Jeb nodded in understanding. "I'm sorry, Tori." His eyes grew thoughtful. "Now that we are engaged, what is keeping us from getting married right away? Then we can rent an apartment together as husband and wife."

"Nothing, I guess. We will simply have to make arrangements with our pastor."

"That should be easy enough. At least, he won't have a problem with our getting married. Let's go talk with him tomorrow."

Tori studied Jeb injured face. "But what about you?" You need to recover first. I'm sure your face hurts quite a bit."

"It does. But it will hurt whether or not we make wedding arrangements. Perhaps keeping busy will take my mind off the pain."

"Are you sure?"

"Perfectly sure."

Tori's heart soared. "Then, after we settle with Pastor Harding, we can start looking for an apartment."

"A delightful idea!"

As the taxi approached her house, Tori's muscles tensed. She couldn't have Pop see her with Jeb. Especially not after the ultimatum Pop had given her.

The taxi driver pulled up in front of Tori's house.

Jeb tapped the driver on the shoulder. "Please wait a moment while I escort my fiancée to her door."

At the sound of the word *fiancée*, Tori's heart leapt with joy. She was Jeb's fiancée, and soon to be his wife. She could have wanted nothing more.

But her joy quickly turned to worry. She placed a hand of restraint on Jeb's arm. "Thank you, Jeb. But you'd better not walk me to my door. Pop may see you, and that would mean big trouble."

"Very well, then." He turned to the cab driver. "Please wait until she is safely inside." Then, taking Tori's hand, Jeb planted a kiss on it. "Until later, my love."

She nodded and gave him a wistful look. "Goodbye, Jeb."

"Very soon, we won't have to say goodbye."

Tori smiled. "Rest well. We are in for a big day."

Tori exited the cab and walked to her door. Just before opening it, she turned and waved goodbye to Jeb.

As the cab left, her heart left with it.

* * * *

After a short sleep, Jeb awakened with a reddened, swollen face and a nagging ache in his cheek. He groaned as he got out of bed, placing his hand to his face to help ease the pain. An ice pack earlier had done little to bring down the swelling that, the doctor had said, could take several days to subside.

Jeb glanced at the clock on his nightstand. Seven-twenty-three a.m. In an hour, he would meet Tori to make arrangements with their pastor to marry them. From there, they would go apartment-hunting in a neighborhood within walking distance of the university.

At the thought of Tori, Jeb's spirits soared. In accepting his marriage proposal, she'd made him the happiest man on earth. Now they could move forward with their lives according to plan and create a bright future together.

He rose, dressed, and drank a cup of tepid coffee, being careful to sip from the uninjured side of his mouth. Several moments later, he was on his way to meet Tori at the little nearby church which she'd attended for several years and which he'd started attending with her shortly after they'd met.

When he arrived, he found her already there, eagerly awaiting him. The church building itself was small and unimposing, with a simple steeple and even simpler architecture. The perfect place for a quiet wedding.

Jeb greeted Tori with a painful smile and a gentle kiss. "Good morning to the future Mrs. Kalitsi. You must be eager to get married."

"I've never wanted anything more in my entire life." Tori embraced him and carefully placed a kiss on his good cheek. "You look better this morning. The swelling has gone down a bit."

He offered her his arm. "Well, shall we go in?"

"Yes." She smiled and took his arm.

They found Pastor Harding in his office, located to the right of the sanctuary. Upon seeing them, the pastor rose and greeted them warmly. "Well, well! Two of my favorite people!" He smiled and looked at Jeb. "What happened to your face?"

Jeb glanced at Tori and looked at the pastor. "Let's just say, there are some people out there who don't like interracial relationships."

"I'm so very sorry to hear you were a victim of that, Jeb. We've had similar problems in this neighborhood, so I understand what you mean. I will pray for you."

"Thanks."

Jeb glanced at Tori and grinned. "We want to get married and would like you to perform the ceremony."

Pastor Harding smiled. "Why, congratulations! It would be my honor. You two have been such a blessing to our church." He motioned them to sit down. "So, when would you like to schedule the big day?"

"This coming Friday, March 4th, if that fits into your schedule."

Pastor Harding checked his desk calendar. "Actually, that day is open. Do you have a specific time in mind?"

Tori leaned forward. "Would four in the afternoon be okay?"

"Yes. That would work well."

She turned toward Jeb. "We could celebrate with dinner right afterward."

Jeb nodded. "Of course, you and your wife are invited, Pastor."

"Thank you. We'd love that!"

Jeb had grown to respect Pastor Harding in Jeb's short time at the church. The man was genuine—a true follower of Jesus Christ.

"Do you have a marriage license?"

"We'll have it in time for the wedding."

Pastor Harding leaned back in his chair. His face grew serious as he steepled his fingers. "Let me be perfectly honest with you. I personally have no problem performing your marriage ceremony. God created all men equal. Unfortunately, our society does not recognize that truth." He paused. "So, I want to warn you that if the public discovers that there will be an interracial marriage here at our church, there may be repercussions."

Jeb grew tense. "What do you mean? We've never had a problem while attending here. In fact, we've felt quite accepted by the congregation."

Pastor Harding nodded. "And I hope you always will feel accepted. Over the years I've been pastor here, I've taught our congregation that racial prejudice is a sin. But the neighborhood outside this church isn't too keen on blacks and whites intermingling, let alone marrying."

Tori leaned forward. "So, what are you saying?"

Pastor Harding leaned his elbows on the desk. "I'm saying that it would be best to keep the wedding as quiet as possible."

Jeb glanced at Tori. "We are not planning to have a big wedding. Actually, it will be only Tori and me, her sister, my best man, and Tori's friend Susanna. Mrs. Harding is invited as well. We can keep things very quiet from the public."

"That would be a good idea. A very good idea. We don't want to arouse any trouble where people could get hurt."

Tori agreed. "Of course not."

Pastor Harding rose. "If you'll please excuse me, I have a meeting with one of our elders in ten minutes." He smiled. "Congratulations on your decision to marry! I'll see you on Friday. And don't forget to bring the marriage license with you." He extended his hand toward Jeb and then Tori.

Jeb made a mental calculation. Today was Saturday. It would take three days to obtain a marriage license. That would be just enough time before the wedding. His heart filled with gratitude. "Is there anything else we need to bring?"

"No. Just yourselves—and your love for each other." Pastor Harding smiled broadly.

Jeb rose. "Thank you, Pastor."

"Oh, one last thing. Because of what I said earlier, come prayed up." His voice was cautionary.

Jeb tensed. Hadn't he and Tori already experienced enough opposition to their relationship? Would they have to face even more? "Thanks for the warning."

Pastor Harding nodded. "Sure thing."

In a few moments, Jeb emerged from the little church, holding Tori's hand fast in his. "There! That's done!"

Tori turned toward him. "Jeb, I'm concerned. What do you think about what Pastor said?"

"I think he's just trying to be cautious." He squeezed her hand. "No need to worry."

But why, deep in his gut, did he have an uneasy feeling that he needed to be on his guard?

Chapter 12

After a late lunch at a nearby Horn & Hardart Restaurant, during which Tori searched the newspaper and made a list of available apartments in the area, she headed with Jeb toward the first rental on the list. It was located only two blocks from the university, in an old, quiet neighborhood.

The late February day was brisk and windy, as they walked, hand in hand, down the brick-covered sidewalks, past a group of children happily playing in a small park along the way.

Tori smiled. One day, she and Jeb would have children of their own. In her mind's eye, she pictured Jeb laughing as he wrestled on the floor with their young son, who would have his father's smile. Or Jeb attending their little girl's tea party, all dressed up in his finest royal costume.

A tender longing overtook Tori. She smiled and waved to the children, who cheerfully waved back at her.

In a few moments, she and Jeb reached the apartment building. It was a modest, three-story brownstone wedged between brownstones on either side. In front of it stood a sign that read *SECOND-FLOOR VACANCY AVAILABLE. INQUIRE WITHIN.*

Tori entered the worn oaken front door, followed by Jeb. To the right, a small office with tall, shaded windows held a wooden desk behind which sat a middle-aged woman who pored over a ledger book.

Upon seeing Tori, the woman rose. "Hello. May I help you?"

"We are here to inquire about the second-floor apartment you have for rent and would like to see it, please."

"Is the apartment just for you?" The woman shot an uneasy look toward Jeb but directed her question at Tori.

Tori glanced at Jeb. "Actually, no. We are going to be married in a few days and would like to rent it for both of us as husband and wife."

The woman's face paled. "I'm sorry, but the apartment has already been rented."

Tori's stomach clenched. "But your sign outside says it's available."

The woman seemed distraught. "Oh, I'm sorry. I forgot to remove the sign."

Tori's face flushed. "I would suggest you remove the sign immediately, as well as your classified advertisement in the newspaper. Otherwise, you could be sued for fraudulent advertising."

The woman's eyes narrowed. "It was an honest mistake." Her voice was clipped. "I will correct it right away."

"I hope you do!"

Her blood boiling, Tori stalked out of the office with Jeb following close behind. So this was the dirty game people would try to play with her and Jeb's lives. Well, they didn't realize they had met their match in Tori.

"The nerve!" Once on the sidewalk, Tori almost spat out the words. "That woman was lying through her teeth!"

Tori sliced the air with the folded newspaper she held in her hand. "I can't believe this! To shun us just because of our skin color!"

"*My* skin color, Tori, not yours. If a white man were with you, she would have rented you the apartment."

Tori's heart broke. "Oh, Jeb! Don't ever say that again! I don't want another man. I want you." She placed her arms around his waist and rested her head on his broad chest.

Every muscle in Tori's body trembled with rage as they made their way to the nearby park. "Jeb, we've got to do something. We can't keep living like this, enduring insult after insult. Isn't there anything we can do to stop it?" Her pulse raced as they crossed the street to the park entrance on the other side.

Taking a deep breath to compose herself, she sat down on a bench by a lovely brook that flowed through the center of the park. Its melodious gurgle soothed her jagged nerves as it meandered over blue-gray rocks and rose-colored pebbles strewn in its bed.

Jeb sat down beside her and took her hand. "Tori, I understand that racism makes you angry."

"Extremely angry." She sighed. "I guess the best thing to do is to pray. Pray for those who abuse us. Pray for those who really don't know what they're doing."

"Exactly."

"Oh, Jeb. I don't care what happens. I don't care how many people come against us. It will only make our love stronger and deeper."

Weary from the emotional pounding of the past few days, she rested her head on his shoulder and prayed a silent prayer for strength.

* * * *

Tori stood in front of the bathroom mirror, staring at her tired face. Her hair was a tangled mess after hours of trudging through litter-laden city streets, riding buses spewing diesel fumes, and dodging dust-laden winds depositing debris in her tresses. Dark rings circled her eyes, and the deep rose lipstick she'd so carefully applied in the morning had all but disappeared. She looked a wreck! It had been a long, tough day. A day that had drained her emotionally and physically, leaving her feeling like a dried-out dishrag.

And poor Jeb! He'd had to deal not only with the emotional challenges of the day, but also with his bruised face that, Tori was sure, still hurt him quite a bit. Although, dear man, he didn't complain once about it the entire day.

She sighed. It seemed as though all the world's prejudice had been compressed into a single portion that day and dumped on them in debilitating doses.

A tear trickled down her cheek. Soon that trickle turned into a torrent of wrenching tears. Like a geyser, sobs shot up from the depths of her soul.

Tori lowered her head and let the tears fall into the sink. With each shed tear, a burden dropped from her soul and a new resolve rose within her, growing stronger and stronger.

Filling her with new life.

Whether or not she and Jeb made it was entirely up to them.

To both of them together. And to each of them separately.

One spouse could be strong when the other was weak. One spouse could be hopeful when the other was in despair. One spouse could save a marriage if that one spouse were determined enough to save it.

Whether or not a marriage lasted was a choice. A choice to consider no other option but to make it last.

A deep peace settled over her soul. She closed her eyes. She wasn't alone. God was with her.

And God would be with her for the rest of her days. When she'd surrendered her life to Him, He'd promised never to leave her nor forsake her. With God's help, she could overcome anything.

With God's help, she and Jeb would make it. Her heart told her so.

When she'd spent all of her tears, she raised her head and looked at her reflection in the mirror. In her now reddened eyes, she saw the real Tori Pendola. The strong young woman who would never allow life to overcome her. The determined young woman who, by God's grace, would prevail against all odds.

The faithful young woman who would love Jeb Kalitsi with all of her life for the rest of her life.

No matter what.

She lifted her chin and stared at her reflection in the mirror. She shook her head. No! Rejection would never destroy her. Tori Pendola would stand up against racism. She would fight its evil lies. She would fight them with all the love that was within her. She would fight them with the truth of God's Word, for only His truth could transform hearts and set people free.

She gazed at her reflection and smiled. It was time to move forward. It was time to marry Jeb.

It was time to prove to herself, to Jeb, and to the world that love never failed.

* * * *

Late that night, Jeb sat on the edge of his bed, tired and sore. Guilt gnawed at him as the recurring nightmare of Kofi's death suffocated him yet again. No matter how much he'd tried over the years to push it aside, the nightmare kept coming back. Haunting him. Accusing him. Whispering its ugly verdict: "You're guilty of Kofi's death. Guilty! Guilty! Guilty!"

Jeb shook his head, trying desperately to dispel the condemning words. But they kept echoing in his soul, robbing him of his peace.

Was he truly guilty of Kofi's death, as Kofi's father had declared at the elder council meeting? Or had he truly done his best to save his best friend against the overpowering forces of nature?

Truth began to dawn in Jeb's heart. Cowardice was taking no action in the face of fear, but he had acted in the face of fear. In the midst of the harrowing storm, he'd done everything humanly possible to save Kofi. He was not responsible for Kofi's death. He'd invited his friend in good faith to go fishing.

He'd intended no harm toward him, only good. That a pleasant event turned into a tragedy was not Jeb's fault, no matter what Kofi's father said.

Jeb took a deep breath as the light of truth began to dispel the dark shadows in his heart. He had an enemy whose sole purpose was to thwart the destiny of those who loved God. This enemy had been trying to thwart Jeb's destiny by pounding him with false guilt.

And Jeb had believed his debilitating lie.

Jeb raked his fingers through his hair. There it was. The truth. As bright as day. He'd assumed a guilt that was not his to assume. A false guilt. And that false guilt had nearly destroyed his life.

His thoughts turned to Tori. Was he assuming a false guilt in regard to her as well? Was he blaming himself for asking her to marry him, knowing full well the difficult life that lay ahead for her? Was he blaming himself for her assault? For the racial slurs she'd endured? For the broken relationship with her father?

He swallowed hard. Yes. He'd been blaming himself. Yet, he was not responsible for Tori's choices. He was not responsible for what happened to her outside of his own actions. He was responsible only to love her to the best of his ability. Nothing more. Nothing less.

Hope rekindled in the depths of Jeb's soul. He straightened, ready to face whatever life brought his way. In His death and resurrection, Jesus had taken Jeb's guilt, whether false or not. Jeb had embraced that truth. And now, with Jesus in his life, he could do all things.

He could love Tori with abandon.

He could love his family and his tribe without retaliation.

He could love his enemies without fear.

Maybe, just maybe, he could even love himself.

Chapter 13

Tori awakened early Monday morning. Her muscles ached from all the walking she and Jeb had done in search of an apartment over the weekend. Today there would be more walking. At least, until they found a place to rent.

Their plans were to remain in the States until Jeb heard from the tribal elder regarding the chieftaincy. Without such a response, it was no use moving to Ghana. At least, not at this point.

Tori rose from her bed and donned her robe. She wanted to catch Anna before her sister left for work. Tori breathed a sigh of relief as she found Anna alone in the living room.

"Anna, I need you to do me a favor."

"Sure. What's up?"

Tori spoke in a low voice, worried that her parents would overhear her. "Saturday, Jeb and I looked at an apartment for rent not far from campus. When the clerk saw we were an interracial couple, she told us the apartment had already been rented, even though the sign outside said the apartment was available."

Anna shook her head. "That's disgusting."

"Exactly what I thought." Tori sighed. "Would you do me a favor and call the rental office today and ask if the apartment is available? I want to know if she was telling us the truth or not."

"I would be delighted to do that." She glanced at her wristwatch. "In fact, I'll call right now. I have a few minutes to spare before I leave for work."

"Thanks so much! Here's the number." Tori handed Anna a small slip of paper with the rental office phone number written on it.

Anna held the receiver loosely against her ear so that Tori could lean in and hear as well. Tori waited for Anna to dial the telephone number.

Anna spoke clearly into the phone's mouthpiece. "Hello. I'm calling to inquire if the apartment you have for rent is still available."

"Yes, it is." The words came through to Tori like lightning before thunder.

And her heart was struck to the core yet again.

"Thank you." Anna hung up before the clerk could ask further questions and turned to Tori, an angry look on her face. "Well, there's your answer."

So the clerk had lied to them. Her sole reason for refusing to rent to them was the color of Jeb's skin.

Bile flooded Tori's throat. "What should I do?"

"I don't know that there's much you can do. It would cost you a pretty penny to sue."

"And would I even stand a chance of winning?"

"I doubt it." Anna grabbed her purse. "Well, I've got to go. Pop will fly through the roof if I'm late."

"Thanks again, Anna."

"Anytime." She gave Tori a hug. "I hope you fare better today in your search for a place to live."

"I hope so, too."

After Anna left, Tori dressed quickly. She had arranged to meet Jeb at the *Penn-Ultimate Café* at 9:00 a.m. to begin their second day of apartment-hunting before her afternoon class.

She found him waiting for her, a smile on his injured face.

"Good morning, Jeb!" Her heart soared at the sight of him, bruise and all.

As she approached their special table, he rose and took both her hands. "Good morning, my love! Whenever you enter a room, the sunshine enters with you."

She gave him a big smile. "You are such the romantic!"

He helped her with her coat and then pulled out a chair for her. When they were both seated, a waitress came to their table.

"Coffee, please, with two blueberry muffins." Jeb ordered the usual for both of them.

The waitress smiled. "I'll be back shortly."

Tori leaned toward Jeb. "Well, you'll never guess what happened this morning."

"What?"

"I had Anna call the rental office at the apartment building we visited Saturday."

"And?"

"And the clerk told Anna that the apartment is still available!"

A cloud crossed Jeb's face. "I'm so sorry, Tori."

"For what? For the foolish prejudice of some people? That's on them. We love each other, Jeb. And that's all that matters."

The waitress returned with their coffee and muffins. After they'd eaten, Jeb paid the tab, left a tip for the waitress, and helped Tori with her coat. "Time to go apartment-hunting again."

Jeb's eyes smiled. "One thing I know for sure. There's no one with whom I'd rather go apartment-hunting than you."

Tori's heart warmed. "The feeling is mutual."

Hand in hand, they exited the café.

But as they left, Tori's stomach sank. What if they never found an apartment? What if no one would rent to an interracial couple? What would they do? Where would they live? In only four days, they would be husband and wife.

But would they be husband and wife without a place to lay their heads?

She remembered Mary and Joseph. On the verge of delivering the Christ Child, they'd had no place to lay their heads. Yet, God had provided for them. The same God would provide for her and Jeb, too.

All she had to do was trust Him.

* * * *

A gust of wind whipped against Jeb's face as he and Tori exited the café. In a few short weeks, spring would arrive in Philadelphia, bringing with it the warmer weather he craved.

He took Tori's hand in his. "I need to stop by the Western Union office this morning to send another telegram to the chief elder."

Tori's brows furrowed. "This will be the third one, right?"

"Yes. If I do not receive a response this time, I will assume that the elders have denied me the chieftaincy."

"I'm so sorry, Jeb."

He squeezed her hand. "No need to be sorry. If that is what they want, that is what they will get."

"But can't you fight for the position? After all, it's yours by inheritance."

"I could." He paused. "But how effective is a leader if his subjects have no respect for him? The people would be better off having the leader they want."

"Then they might see what they've given up."

"I suppose so." Jeb's stomach clenched. If he were totally honest with himself, the chief elder's failure to respond to him aroused his ire. Even if the tribe had voted against him, they should at least have the decency to notify him. It would be critical to know if he and Tori would be making their home in the States or in Ghana.

As it stood, he would proceed on the assumption that the elders did not want him and that he and Tori should look for a place to live here in the States.

He looked at her and smiled. "So, where to, milady?"

Tori held up the page she'd torn from the newspaper. "I circled the available apartments in the campus area that were listed in Sunday's paper. There's a two-bedroom apartment that would provide us with an extra room to use as an office. It's only a block from campus."

"Yes. That sounds good. Let's look at that one first."

The morning air bristled with life. Aided by the appetizing aroma of their wares, street vendors, standing beside their food carts, peddled coffee, doughnuts, and egg sandwiches. Hungry businessmen, toting leather briefcases, stopped for a quick meal before beginning a busy day. On nearly every street corner, young boys, pitching the morning paper, shouted to passersby to get the latest news.

Jeb stopped, gave the paperboy a dime, and received the morning edition of *The Philadelphia Inquirer* in return. "Today's edition might feature some new apartment listings."

Tori nodded. "Yes. Good idea."

After a few moments, they reached the first apartment on their list. It was on the second floor, facing the back of the building.

Jeb followed Tori into the rental office.

A young man stood at the reception desk. "Good morning." He gave Jeb a questioning look. "How may I help you?"

Tori greeted the man. "We are here to look at the second-floor apartment you have listed for rent."

The man hesitated. "Is it for both of you?"

"Yes. We will be married soon and need a place to live."

"I see." The man paused, furrowing his brows. 'I don't recall that the landlord listed a second-floor apartment for rent."

"Perhaps I made a mistake. Perhaps it is on some other floor." Tori showed the man the newspaper and pointed to the listing. "It's right here. I've circled it."

The man glanced at the newspaper listing. "Well, it's there all right." His face turned crimson. "Please give me a moment to check." He left the reception area and went into a back office.

Jeb gave Tori a knowing look. They'd been through enough of these excuses together to recognize them a mile away.

The man soon returned. "I'm sorry, but that listing is a mistake. We have no apartments available."

Jeb was about to explode. "I see." He took in a deep breath. "Do you know of any apartments available in this area? We are both students and need to be near the University."

"I'm afraid not."

Jeb swallowed the bile in his throat. "Very well, then. Thank you."

"You're welcome."

As Jeb led Tori out of the office, the man called to them. "I hope you find something."

But the man's words dissipated in the rising anger that filled Jeb's soul.

Once outside, he vented to Tori. "I wish we could sue."

"Well, legally, we could."

"But the legal fees would be exorbitant." He sighed. "Besides, given the public sentiment, we'd be hard pressed to win the case."

"Plus, you're a foreigner, remember. I'm not sure what recourse you would have in this country."

He nodded. Feeling helpless was something Jeb neither liked nor was accustomed to. He'd always been a take-charge person, grabbing the bull by the horns and subduing it. To find himself in a powerless position gnawed at his gut. "What's the next apartment on your list?"

"A studio apartment on Samson Street."

"A studio? Don't you think that would be a bit small?"

"Yes. But it may be the only thing we can get close to campus. Shall we look at it?"

"Yes. Let's go."

The studio apartment was located three blocks from the one they'd just visited. A bit farther from campus, but still within walking distance.

"There it is!" Tori pointed to the red brick building a few yards away. "The rental office is on the first floor."

Jeb led Tori into the building, a sinking feeling settling in his stomach. Would they meet with the same response? The same refusal?

The same rejection?

As they entered the rental office, a female clerk greeted them. "What can I do for you?"

Tori smiled. "We would like to look at the studio apartment you have for rent."

"Oh, I'm so sorry. We just rented it to a student from Penn."

Jeb intervened. "Very interesting. Then why is it still listed in this morning's newspaper?"

The woman grew flustered. "I don't know. It's possible that the landlord forgot to pull the ad."

Jeb clenched his jaw. "Or is it possible that your landlord does not want to rent to a black-and-white couple?"

The woman averted her eyes. "I can't speak for what the landlord wants or doesn't want."

Jeb took Tori by the arm. "Let's go. I see that we are not wanted here, either."

He led Tori toward the door.

Would they ever be wanted anywhere?

* * * *

A knock on the door in the early hours of the morning aroused Jeb. He raked his fingers through his hair, trying to clear the fogginess in his brain, then rose and reached for his robe. Who could be knocking on his door at this hour of the morning? And why?

Jeb opened the door to find a young man standing in the hall, holding an envelope in his right hand.

"Western Union here, sir. Are you Jebuni Kalitsi?"

Jeb nodded. "Yes. I am Jebuni."

The carrier handed him the telegram. "I'm sorry for disturbing you so early, but telegrams are usually urgent."

Jeb's pulse quickened. "It's no problem. Thank you very much."

"You're welcome. Good day to you."

"Good day to you as well."

Jeb closed the door. His heart pounded as he made his way to the kitchen table and sat down. The morning sun cast its first rays through the kitchen window, lifting the shadows of night as it bid them farewell for another day. Would that the sun could lift the ominous dread that now troubled his heart.

Kelechi ambled into the kitchen, holding his head with both hands. "Hey, man! Who had the nerve to wake me out of a beautiful dream?" He drew up to Jeb's side, his hair disheveled and his voice groggy.

"Western Union."

"Oh!" Kelechi snapped into wakefulness. "What's up, man?"

"I got a telegram from Ghana."

Kelechi backed away. "Would you like me to leave while you read it?"

Jeb looked up at him. "No. Please stay. I may need your moral support."

His hands trembling, Jeb tore open the telegram and read:

To Jebuni Kalitsi:

We regret to inform you that the elders have voted against your assuming the tribal chieftaincy and have, instead, decided to assign the stool to your brother Adofo.

We wish you well.

Siisi Odamtten, Chief Elder

A knife sliced Jeb's heart, choking the breath out of him. It was insult enough to refuse him his rightful inheritance, but to bestow it upon his younger brother was beyond insult. It was nothing short of humiliating.

The blood rushed from Jeb's face as he sat in a stupor. Had Adofo wanted the chieftaincy all along? Had he envied Jeb's firstborn position and desired the birthright for himself? Had he schemed his way into this decision?

Jeb and Adofo had never gotten along very well, despite Jeb's many efforts to ingratiate himself to his younger brother. But Jeb had never imagined that Adofo's jealousy would lead to his stealing his brother's birthright. Never once had Adofo mentioned his desire to be chief. Had he hidden this desire?

"Jeb, what is it?" Kelechi sat beside him, concern on his face.

Dazed, Jeb handed the telegram to his friend.

Kelechi read the message and shook his head. "This is a disgrace!"

Jeb stood and paced the floor. "It is more than a disgrace. It is an abomination. A gross usurpation of tribal protocol. An insult of the highest order against my deceased father."

Kelechi handed the telegram back to Jeb. "Is there anything you can do about it?"

Jeb fisted his palms. "Yes. And I will."

Never in his wildest imaginations would he have thought that the chieftaincy would go to his brother. First of all, Jeb was the firstborn. Second, Adofo was young and inexperienced. Third, he'd done nothing to prove himself worthy of being chief.

"Jeb, I know you're hurting at the injustice."

"I'm not only hurting. I'm seething with rage. And to think that this was all done behind my back! And possibly by my own brother." His voice rose several decibels.

Kelechi placed a hand on Jeb's shoulder. "Are you sure it happened as you think? That your brother planned this?"

Kelechi's question caught Jeb off guard. "I don't know how else it could have happened."

"Does anyone else have anything against you?"

Jeb thought a moment. "Yes. The father of my young friend Kofi who drowned in the storm while we were fishing."

"I remember your telling me about that."

"Yafeu is the only one, other than my brother, who has something against me. I never knew that, however, until the council meeting."

"Then could it be that Yafeu is behind all of this?"

Jeb considered Kelechi's words. "It could be. After all, he did accuse me of killing his son, so he could have recommended my brother as an act of vengeance against me. But I'm not sure." Jeb sat back down again. "I've been betrayed, Kelechi. Utterly betrayed."

Kelechi placed a hand on Jeb's shoulder. "Betrayal is a brutal thing."

Jeb nodded. "There is nothing more brutal."

"I wish there were something I could do for you."

Jeb rose again. "I need to talk to Tori." She would give him much needed perspective. Much needed understanding.

Much needed advice.

"I think that is a good idea." Kelechi paused. "I'll be leaving for class soon, so you'll have some privacy."

"Thanks." Jeb rose. His head throbbed. Although he'd been willing to give up the chieftaincy for Tori, to have it wrenched out of his clasp was demeaning, but to have it given over to his brother was even worse. It was not only a debilitating blow to Jeb's ego, but also a savage blow to his heart.

Would he ever recover?

He dialed Tori's number, unmindful of the early hour.

"Hello." A man's voice answered the phone.

Jeb panicked. It was Tori's father.

What was Jeb thinking by calling her at this time of day?

"I'm sorry, sir. I apologize …"

"Next time, be more careful! It's only 6:30 in the morning, and you woke me up!"

And with that, Tori's father slammed down the phone before Jeb could ask for Tori, leaving him no choice but to talk with her later.

Chapter 14

Tori awakened at the crack of dawn after a restless night. She and Jeb were to be married in two days, and they still had not found a place to live. Would today's apartment-hunting bring the same disappointment? The same rejection?

The same hypocrisy?

She rose, grabbed her pink chenille robe from the chair, and tiptoed out of the bedroom so as not to awaken Anna.

To Tori's surprise, Pop sat at the kitchen table, drinking coffee.

"Good morning, Pop."

"Good morning." Pop grunted. "What are you doing up so early?"

Tori chuckled. "I guess I could ask you the same question."

Pop scowled. "Some idiot called at 6:30 this morning. Said he had a wrong number. Woke me out of a deep sleep. Sounded like a foreigner. He spoke with an accent."

Tori panicked. "What kind of accent?"

"Like those English people from England."

Tori's stomach churned. Could the caller have been Jeb? If so, he must have received word about the chieftaincy.

"I'm sorry your sleep was disturbed, Pop."

"Well, worse things have happened." He rose and put his empty coffee cup in the sink. "Do you have classes today?"

"Not until this afternoon." Tori's muscles tensed. She still hadn't told Pop that she and Jeb were going to be married. Maybe she should do so now and get it over with. Pop would find out sooner or later anyway. Better that the news come directly from her.

"Pop?"

"Yeah. What is it, Tori?" His voice sounded annoyed.

"I have something to tell you." She paused. "You won't like it, but I'd rather tell you myself than have you find out some other way."

Pop's gaze was locked on hers. "Just say it, Tori."

"Jeb and I are going to be married."

"You're what?" Fire flared in Pop's eyes.

"We're going to be married."

"So, you decided just like that? Without asking my opinion or permission?"

"I already know your opinion. You don't want me to marry a black man."

"Not only do I not want you to marry a black man, I *forbid* you to marry a black man."

Tori bit her tongue. She didn't want to say anything she would later regret. "Pop, I'm twenty-four years old. I no longer need your permission. I am an adult and have the right to make my own decisions."

Pop's face turned red. "Okay. If that's the way you want it. From now on, you can forget about being my daughter. I want nothing more to do with you." With that, he got up and left.

Tori's body shook as a sob lodged in her throat, silencing the voice of her soul. She was as one dead. Lifeless. Breathless.

Numb.

Her head spinning, she steadied herself against the kitchen table, gasping for air. All of her life she'd hoped that maybe one day Pop would accept her. Would want her.

Would love her.

But now he'd crushed that hope and left her in the certainty that she was, indeed, unwanted. Unloved.

An accident.

She swallowed hard and drew in a deep breath. There was only one thing to do. Be strong. Move forward.

Leave the past—and Pop—behind.

The sound of the front door slamming shut told her Pop had left for work.

She made her way into the living room to call Jeb.

His voice at the other end of the line sounded troubled. "Jeb, what's wrong?"

"A telegram arrived this morning."

She braced herself for the news.

"I have been deposed as chief."

"Oh, Jeb! I'm so sorry!"

"But the worst of it is that my brother has been chosen in my stead."

Tori's heart nearly stopped. "I can't believe it!"

"Neither can I."

Her heart wrenched for Jeb. He, too, had been rejected.

"What are you going to do?" She wanted so much to take away his pain.

"I don't know. I need to talk with you."

"I can be at the café in an hour."

"Yes. Let's meet there. I have much to discuss with you."

"I love you, Jeb."

"I love you, too, Tori."

Tori dressed quickly and caught the bus to the Penn campus. The early March day was cool and brisk. Perfect for apartment-hunting.

But would the telegram from Ghana change all that? Would Jeb choose to fight for his birthright? Would he have to return to his homeland to do so?

Would he change his mind about marrying her?

Icy panic blew through Tori's veins. No. Jeb would never go back on his word. Never.

The bus stopped at the corner near the café. After she descended the steps to exit, she held her breath so as not to breathe in the exhaust fumes that always hung in the air after the bus's departure.

She hurried toward the café. Along the sidewalk's edge, two orange crocuses stood at attention in the soil, heralding the arrival of spring. On the low branch of a budding oak, a tree swallow trilled its morning song.

A spark of hope surged in Tori's heart. The hope of a new beginning.

She longed to put everything behind her and begin anew. To erase the past and start with a clean slate.

But could she?

She'd soon find out.

She found Jeb waiting for her at their usual table in the back of the café. He stood to greet her. His face was strained. Sullen.

She embraced him. "Tell me what is going on."

He helped her with her chair and then took his place across the table from her. In a tone of voice she'd never heard him use before, he began. "I must go back to Ghana."

Jeb's words punched Tori right in the middle of her gut. What did his decision to return to Ghana mean for him? For her?

For them?

Was he saying that their engagement was off? That their marriage would never take place?

That he and Tori would part ways forever?

He seemed to read her thoughts. "And I want you to go back with me as my wife."

Tori's heart roller-coasted from despair to joy in a single moment.

Jeb took her hand. "I have decided to fight for the chieftaincy. I cannot stand back and allow such injustice to prevail. I will contend for the chieftain's stool." He squeezed her hand. "Will you stand with me, Tori?"

The words flew out of her mouth. And out of her heart. "Yes, Jeb! I will stand with you forever."

Tears welled up in his eyes. "If you only knew how much I love you!"

"So, when do you—I mean, we—leave?"

"The day after our wedding."

Tori's heart lurched. "You mean three days from now?"

"Yes. Friday we marry. The next day we leave for Ghana. Can you manage such a quick departure?"

Tori swallowed hard. She'd have only three days to prepare. What about her studies? Her parents? And what about Anna? Could she do this to Anna?

She sighed. "How long do you think we will be there?"

"Long enough to regain the chieftaincy."

"But, Jeb, what if that takes weeks? Months? Years, even?"

He lowered his eyes. "Would you prefer to join me later?"

"Oh, no, Jeb! I want to be there to support you while you're contending for your office."

She locked her gaze onto his. In his eyes she saw anger. Fear. Worry. His emotions were clouding his thinking.

"Jeb, let's think this through. We both have only a few weeks before we graduate. If we leave now, we would forfeit the entire semester's work. What if we waited to leave until the end of the semester? We would then have our degrees in hand and be free to go."

"But if I wait, it might be too late. My brother's installation could take place any day now." He lowered his voice. "If it has not already taken place."

"And if it has? Do you stand a chance of a decision reversal?"

Jeb rubbed his forehead. "I must go, Tori. I will have no peace if I do not go." His gaze was upon her. "Perhaps it would be better if you remain here. I am afraid that tensions will run high while I am there. I would not want to put you in any danger."

"Does this mean we will have to postpone our wedding?"

He took her hands. "Oh, no, dearest one! We will marry on Friday as planned. After all we've been through to make the arrangements, we cannot back out now. We'll get married Friday. Then the next day I will leave for Ghana."

Tori's heart broke. "When do you think you will be back?"

"I don't know. I will send a telegram to the chief elder informing him that I oppose the council's decision and will contest it. I will tell him to expect me within the week. I'll also send a telegram to my mother to tell her of our marriage and to expect me."

"Are you sure about this, Jeb? I mean, can it not wait until the end of the semester?"

"Tori, it's difficult for me to explain. But this is a matter of honoring my father's wishes. Of honoring my family history.

"Of fighting against injustice."

He held her hands. "I simply must take care of it immediately."

Tori swallowed her grief. "Very well, then. Do what you must."

He tried to cheer her. "Friday will be our wedding day. We will make it a wonderful day!"

She managed a smile. "Yes. We will make it a wonderful day. We will live in the moment and not worry about the next day."

"That is the way our Lord wants us to live. Did He not command us not to worry about tomorrow's troubles because today has enough troubles of its own?"

Tori nodded. Yes, the Lord did make that command. So, despite her sorrow, she would obey it.

But it seemed as though each day's troubles were growing worse than the troubles of the day before. Was evil cumulative? Would she have no respite? No peace?

She forced herself back to the moment. "Our first order of business now is to find a place to live."

"Yes. Let's go." Jeb called the waitress for the bill and paid it.

Tori took his arm as they left the café. "I found an apartment listing in the newspaper last night that seems to be just what we need."

They walked the five blocks to the apartment. It was housed in an old brick home only a stone's throw from the university. "Jeb, I have an idea. I want to do an experiment. I'll wait here while you go in first."

"What's your experiment?"

"I want to see if they refuse you and then rent to me when I apply after you."

"Good idea." Jeb went inside to talk with the clerk while Tori waited outside and out of sight.

In a few moments, Jeb rejoined her, shaking his head. "The apartment has been rented." He paused. "Or so I was told."

Tori's ire flared. "My turn now."

"I hope you fare better than I."

"I have a hunch I will."

Tori entered the building and found the reception clerk. "I saw your sign outside about the apartment for rent. Is it still available?"

"Yes. I'll be happy to show it to you."

"Thank you. But first, I'd like to call my fiancé. He's waiting nearby."

"Of course."

Tori went outside to get Jeb. She gave him a knowing look. "The apartment is available. Would you like to see it?"

"Yes."

When Tori returned with Jeb, the clerk's face turned ashen. She could not find her tongue.

Tori confronted her. "So, why did you lie to my fiancé?"

"I … uh … was just following orders."

Tori's face was on fire. "You lied!"

The clerk regained her composure. "Look. The landlord is against renting to colored people."

"Why didn't you come right out and say that in the beginning?"

"I'm sorry. I should have."

"Well, you and your landlord can have your apartment. You're nothing but hypocrites. The two of you!"

With that, Tori stomped out of the office with Jeb close behind her.

Once outside, she sighed. "Same old story everywhere we go."

Jeb took her by the hand. "Maybe it turned out for the best, Tori. If I regain my chieftaincy, we won't need an apartment. We'll live in Ghana."

"That's true. But where will I live in the meantime? My father said he would disown me if I married you, so I doubt he'll let me live at home."

"Are you kidding me?"

"No. Those were his exact words to me this morning as he left for the office."

Jeb shook his head. "Do you think your father would reconsider?"

Tori shuddered. "I don't know. I could ask him, I guess. But there's no guarantee he will agree."

"Perhaps Anna can intercede for you."

Dear, precious Anna. "I could ask her to intercede for me. But there's no guarantee Pop will change his mind."

Jeb grew pensive. "Do you have a friend with whom you can stay for a short while?"

Tori thought for a moment. "Yes. I can ask Susanna. She is in one of my art classes. She may be able to help me."

"Please give her a call today. I would rest better knowing you will have a roof over your head while I am gone."

Tori knew better than to ask Jeb to reconsider his departure. When something burned deep inside him, there was no putting the fire out. Truth be told, she was glad about that. It meant that the fire that burned deep inside Jeb for her would never be put out.

He took her hand. "Tori, I promise you that one day I will give you the house of your dreams."

She locked her gaze onto his. "Jebuni Kalitsi, I don't care where we live as long as I live with you."

Right there, in the middle of the sidewalk and in broad daylight, Tori kissed him.

And she didn't even care who noticed.

* * * *

The morning of Tori's wedding day loomed bright, blue, and bittersweet. A cloudless sky covered the city. The forecast called for temperatures in the high fifties, unusual for early March, but perfect for a wedding day.

But while the weather was perfect, Tori's heart ached. Pop and Mom had refused to attend the ceremony simply because their daughter had chosen to marry a black man. Despite Tori's pleading, they'd remained adamant in their refusal.

Since she was a little girl, Tori had looked forward to the day her father would walk her down the aisle. But now that the day had arrived, instead of walking her down the aisle, Pop had disowned her.

The old specter of rejection reared its ugly face again, casting a shadow on Tori's mood.

And Mom? Well, Mom had chosen to go along with Pop. Although she was less prejudiced than he, she was still prejudiced.

A drop of arsenic in pure water still made for poisoned water.

Tori swallowed the lump in her throat. She'd look on the good side of things. There was always a good side to every situation, if one only looked for it. Sometimes one had to look very hard.

The good side of her situation was that, in a short while, she would marry the love of her life. The hero of her dreams.

The man God had ordained to be her husband.

Accompanied by Anna and Kelechi, Tori and Jeb reached the little church just before 4:00 p.m., as agreed upon earlier with their pastor. The ceremony would take only a few moments, and they would leave before arousing any attention.

Pastor Harding greeted them warmly. "Good to see you two!"

Jeb introduced him to Kelechi and Anna.

Pastor Harding then led the small party into the sanctuary and positioned himself before the altar. The wedding party took their places in front of him. Susanna and the pastor's wife were the only other guests.

Jeb looked so handsome in his black suit, crisp white shirt, and red tie. On his lapel, he sported a lovely white carnation that Tori had given him. His gaze upon her warmed her heart.

Tori glanced at Anna, standing to her left, an encouraging smile on her face.

Pastor Harding turned first to Jeb. "Please repeat after me."

Jeb repeated the words. "I, Jebuni Kalitsi, take you, Victoria Pendola, to be my lawful wife, to have and to hold, from this day forward, for better, for worse, for richer, for poorer, in sickness and in health, to love and to cherish, till death do us part, according to God's holy ordinance; and thereto I pledge myself to you."

His hand trembling, Jeb slipped a simple gold wedding band onto Tori's ring finger.

Then the pastor turned to Tori. "Please repeat after me."

"I, Victoria Pendola, take you, Jebuni Kalitsi, to be my lawful husband, to have and to hold, from this day forward, for better, for worse, for richer, for poorer, in sickness and in health, to love and to cherish, till death do us part, according to God's holy ordinance; and thereto I pledge myself to you."

Tears welling up in her eyes, Tori placed a matching gold wedding band onto Jeb's ring finger.

Pastor Harding smiled broadly. "I now pronounce you husband and wife." He then invited Jeb to kiss his new bride.

Anna, Kelechi, Susanna, and Mrs. Harding burst into applause.

Just as quickly as it had begun, the ceremony was over. Tori's heart was full. After so many trials and much suffering, she and Jeb were now married. She could now call herself Mrs. Jebuni Kalitsi.

As the small group exited the church, a few people stood outside, shouting obscenities at them.

Suddenly a stone flew their way.

Then several stones.

Tori ducked.

Jeb grabbed her by the shoulders. "Quick. Back inside." Jeb held the door open and waited for everyone to enter. He then followed close behind and shut the door.

Pastor and Mrs. Harding were still in the sanctuary. Pastor Harding looked up, a question on his face.

Jeb explained. "Pastor, a few people outside threw stones at us as we left the church."

A worried look crossed Pastor Harding's face. "I'll need to call the police."

Jeb agreed. "I'm sorry this has happened."

"I'm not surprised, given the prejudicial attitude of this neighborhood. If you recall, I mentioned as much to you when we spoke earlier." Pastor Harding left for his office to call the police.

Tori sat down in the nearest chair and put her face in her hands. She certainly didn't want her pastor to suffer negative repercussions just because he'd officiated at their wedding ceremony. But, there was nothing she could do about it now. She'd barely escaped being struck by a stone. What would be next?

In a few moments, the police arrived. "What's going on?"

Pastor Harding explained the situation. "These are two of my congregants, and I had just performed their wedding ceremony."

While one of the police officers went outside to investigate, the other officer questioned the wedding party and requested a form of identification from each of them in order to write up a report.

Jeb retrieved his passport from his jacket pocket and handed it to the officer.

"Ghana?" The officer looked up at Jeb. "You're here on a student visa?"

"Yes, sir."

"Are you the groom?"

Jeb nodded and smiled.

"Congratulations!" He shook Jeb's hand.

He moved on to Tori. "And I guess you're the bride."

Tori smiled. "Congratulations to you, too."

The other officer returned. "The few miscreants are gone. There was no one to question."

Anna clapped her hands. "And now, on to *The Palm* for the wedding dinner of the century!"

Tori laughed. "Thanks to you, Anna!" Anna's wedding gift to Tori and Jeb was a full-course meal at one of Philadelphia's finest restaurants.

Having finished their report, the police officers accompanied them to their waiting taxicab and then escorted the cab to the restaurant.

Chapter 15

The afternoon after his wedding day, Jeb found himself once again on a plane bound for Ghana. His heart heavy at leaving his new bride, he purposed to accomplish his mission as quickly as possible and return to Tori's waiting arms as the new chief of his tribe.

But accomplishing that mission would take a miracle.

He'd notified the chief elder by telegram of his imminent return. He'd also notified his mother.

Neither one had responded.

What would he find when he got there? Would the trip turn out to be futile? Confrontational?

Unproductive?

Jeb dismissed the negative thoughts from his mind. The chieftaincy was his by birthright. It could not be denied him without clear proof that he was unqualified.

And that clear proof had not been forthcoming.

Yes, Yafeu, Kofi's father, had accused Jeb of cowardice. But no one had been in that storm with him to vouch for any such trait.

No. The real reason for rejecting him as chief was racial prejudice. Pure and simple. The tribe did not want their chief to marry a white woman. Whites represented the enemy. Whites represented subjugation.

Whites represented oppression.

Jeb gripped the arms of his chair as the plane hit some turbulence. He shifted in his seat, trying to calm his already jagged nerves, and focused his attention on planning the best strategy for handling the race situation with his tribe.

First, he would start with his mother. As the wife of the former chief, she held great sway over the tribal council. If Jeb could convince her of the foolishness of her prejudice, she would then convince the council of the foolishness of theirs.

Jeb would appeal to Mama's faith. She was, after all, a Christian. And a Christian, by definition, believed in the equality of all people before God. So, for her to oppose Jeb's marriage to a white woman would be to go contrary to her Christian beliefs.

Mama could not have possibly seen the situation in that light. Surely, she would not willingly contradict God. No. Mama was being controlled by her cultural upbringing. By traditions.

By the lie.

Once she recognized the lie, she would renounce it.

As for the tribe, now that Tori was his wife, the elders could no longer harass him about choosing a wife for him. His marriage was a *fait accompli*. The real issue—racism—was now the only issue he needed to deal with.

He looked out the window. A bank of gray clouds roiled beneath the aircraft. In the distance, the sky grew dark as the aircraft flew toward the Ghanaian time zone. In a few short hours, he would land in Accra and then once again make his way to Sekondi-Takoradi and his parental home.

* * * *

It was nearly six o'clock when Jeb arrived at his mother's house. To his surprise, she had dinner waiting for him.

"Mama, I am home again and glad to see you."

She embraced him warmly. "It is good to have you back, Jebuni."

Her receptive demeanor took Jeb off guard. Something had happened to her between his last visit home and now. But what?

"It is good to be back."

She sat down, and Jeb followed suit.

Mama folded her hands in her lap. "First, I must ask your forgiveness for my unloving behavior on your previous visit. I was unkind and did not act in the love of Christ. Second, I must congratulate you on your marriage."

He braced himself. "Thank you, Mama." He paused. "I know you were not pleased with my choice of wife."

"This is true."

"But I know you will love her."

Mama nodded. "I will make every effort to be kind to her despite the fact that you have broken with tradition." She smiled. "You were always a determined child. And you have become a determined man, bent on achieving your every goal."

Jeb shifted in his chair. "That is the reason I have returned, Mama. To contend for the chieftaincy."

Mama slowly nodded. "I understand."

"To say that I was stunned when I learned that the chieftaincy had been bestowed on Adofo would be an understatement."

"I knew you would be stunned."

Jeb leaned forward. "Please tell me what happened. While I love my brother, I cannot allow him—nor anyone else—to steal the chieftaincy from me. I am Papa's rightful heir, and I must fulfill my obligations. That is what Papa would want."

Mama nodded again and then sighed. "Jebuni, much has been going on behind the scenes since you left so abruptly the last time."

Jeb caught the hint of reprimand in her voice for his sudden departure on his last trip home. "I have all night to listen."

Mama leaned back in her chair. "To begin with, even prior to your father's death, some of the tribal elders were at odds about your succeeding him as chief."

Jeb's eyes widened. "I did not know this."

"Yes. One of the elders—Kofi's father, Yafeu—was especially opposed to your being chief."

"So, that is the reason, during the interview, he accused me of cowardice in the death of his son."

"Precisely." Mama sighed.

Jeb shook his head. Why, then, for so many years, did he seem not to hold Jeb responsible for Kofi's death? It was a rhetorical question.

Mama's voice broke through Jeb's thoughts. "But there is more. Your brother did not want you to succeed as chief, either. Sadly, he allowed jealousy to penetrate his heart and take root there." Mama's gaze fell to her folded hands and then rose again. "As Satan would have it, Yafeu befriended Adofo under the guise of mentoring him, and the two arranged a scheme to deprive you of the chieftaincy. Because of your brother's innate naïveté, Yafeu was able to convince him that he would make a better chief than you. And because of Yafeu's powerful influence as a longstanding elder, he was also able to convince the entire tribal council."

The words sliced Jeb's heart. He shook his head. "I can't believe this!"

Mama sighed. "And all of this was going on right under our noses."

Jeb furrowed his brows. "When did you first learn of this, Mama?"

"I first grew suspicious shortly after you left the last time. Adofo made a comment that caught my attention. He said that since you no longer qualified to be chief, the tribe should consider him because he is also his father's son." Mama stroked her chin. "I found that comment unusual for your brother. He has never been an ambitious young man. For him suddenly to want the chieftaincy seemed out of character for him." She lowered her voice. "I had a feeling there was more going on than met the eye."

Jeb pondered his mother's words. "So, tell me. If the firstborn cannot fill the position of chief, does tribal protocol permit the second-born son to do so?"

"The only time I have heard of such a concession is if the firstborn son dies. Otherwise, the second-born son has no rights to the chieftaincy."

"I see." He steadied his gaze on Mama. "So what happens now? Has Adofo been installed yet?"

"No. But the installation is scheduled for the day after tomorrow. You have arrived just in time."

Jeb raked his fingers through his hair. What should he do? Were it anyone else but this brother usurping the stool, he could handle it easily. But to stand against his own brother? What would that do to their already strained relationship? To the family?

To the tribe?

He had to make a decision.

And he had only a very short time in which to make it.

* * * *

The Monday after her wedding day, Tori carried the last box of her belongings from the hotel where she and Jeb had spent their wedding night into Susanna's tiny apartment. Her friend and classmate had agreed to allow Tori to stay with her until she found an apartment of her own.

Tori hoped that would be very soon.

She dropped the heavy box onto the cot in the tiny spare bedroom and sat down to catch her breath. What a way to start married life! Apart from her husband and living with a friend!

Tori's heart ached as she glanced at her wristwatch. Her new bridegroom was on the other side of the Atlantic. This should have been their honeymoon. All of her youthful dreams about a beautiful wedding—a ceremony in a lovely church, escorted down the aisle by her proud father; admired by her happy, crying mother; followed by a huge reception banquet and then an amazing honeymoon on a tropical island—all of those dreams had vanished into thin air.

Instead, here she was, alone again, and not even in her own house. It wouldn't have been so bad if her father had permitted her to stay at his house while Jeb was gone.

But Pop had disowned her.

Tori swallowed hard. No. She wouldn't give in to self-pity. She'd look for an apartment and make the best of the situation until Jeb's return.

"Do you need any help?" Susanna stood at the doorway.

"No, thanks. I just brought in my last box."

Susanna sat down on the cot next to Tori. "I'm so sorry things have turned out the way they have."

"I am, too. But I'm so thankful to you for allowing me to stay here for a few days. I don't know what I would have done. I promise you I'll get out of your hair as quickly as I can. I'm going out in a little while to look for an apartment."

"Tori, you know you can stay here as long as you need to."

"Yes, I know. But I don't want to take advantage of your kind hospitality." She paused. "Jeb should be back soon. I'm praying the situation with the chieftaincy will be resolved quickly."

Susanna nodded. "What happens if Jeb is accepted as chief?"

"I'll move to Ghana, and we'll live there. If he's not accepted as chief, we'll live here in the States."

Susanna rose. "Whatever happens, you're welcome to stay here in the interim."

"Thanks, Susanna. You're a good friend."

"Well, I've got to get to class. See you later today."

After Susanna left, Tori unpacked her belongings, showered, and dressed. She then set out on another morning of apartment-hunting. She had a feeling that today she'd have no problem renting one.

Newspaper in hand, Tori boarded the bus for the Penn campus and headed for a new listing she'd found just that morning. The bus let her off two blocks from the apartment.

She took a deep breath of the brisk March air. The day bordered on warm as it began its transition toward spring. Here and there, dogwood trees had begun to bud. A few graced the neighborhood where she now walked, encouraging her heart.

Spring always reminded her of God's faithfulness. He delighted in making things new. Was she willing to trust Him to make things new in her life as well? Was she willing to trust Him with her future, no matter what that future looked like?

Tori approached the three-story row house that served as an apartment building. She entered the front door and found herself in a tall-ceilinged room with two large windows. A woman sat at a desk at the far end of the room.

"Good morning. May I help you?" The woman rose.

Tori approached the desk. "Yes. I'm here to look at the apartment you have for rent on the second floor."

"Wonderful!" The woman reached into a desk drawer and removed a cluster of keys. "Please follow me."

Tori accompanied her to the second floor. "Are you from around here?"

"Yes. I'm a graduate student at Penn."

"Oh, I see."

"Will you be renting alone?"

What should Tori say? Yes, she would be renting alone, but her husband would be living with her. "Do you mean will the apartment be in my name only?"

The woman stopped. "No. I mean will you be the only one living here?"

"Actually, no. My husband will be joining me soon."

The woman gave her a strange look. "I see." She then unlocked the door.

As Tori entered the spacious front room, her heart leapt. The room was bright and cheery. Sunshine splashed across the hardwood floor and seemed to fill every corner of the space. A second room behind the first one revealed a small dining area. Behind that sat a tiny, modern kitchen, complete with a cooking stove, a refrigerator, and several large cabinets. To the side of the kitchen was a single large bedroom with a tall window facing the back of the building.

Tori liked what she saw. "This will do perfectly."

The woman smiled. "Very well, then. We can draw up a contract now and the apartment will be yours."

Tori followed the woman to the office on the first floor.

"Here is the application. You may sit at that table while you fill it out."

As Tori answered the questions, one in particular jumped out at her: *Please indicate your race and the race of other occupants of the apartment: White / Colored / Mixed.*

Tori's muscles tensed. In a single stroke, she crossed out all three words and replaced them with the word *Human.* Then she returned the application to the woman.

The woman scanned the application. "I'm sorry, but you must choose one of the answers regarding race."

Utterly disgusted, Tori took the application back from the woman and tore it up right in front of her. "You can have your lovely apartment—and your stinking prejudice as well. I want no parts of either."

With that, Tori stalked out of the building.

Would there ever be a place where she and Jeb could live together?

Chapter 16

The next morning, after talking with Mama and asking the Holy Spirit for strategy, Jeb decided that the best course of action would be to confront Adofo directly before confronting anyone else. He would approach his brother in love, but also in truth, as the Scriptures commanded.

Adofo lived in his own house only a short distance from their mother. As Jeb drove there in his rented car, the hot Ghanaian sun beat down upon the expansive fields on either side of the dirt road.

A lump formed in Jeb's throat. How he loved this land of his birth! How he longed to share it with Tori!

How he missed her!

Had he been wrong in leaving her so abruptly after their wedding? Had he been selfish? Had he broken her heart?

But what other choice had he had? If he were to fight for the chieftaincy, he had to do it immediately. Otherwise, he would lose it forever.

And to lose it forever would have serious consequences for himself, Tori, his family, and his tribe.

When Jeb reached his brother's house, he found Adofo sitting on the veranda.

Jeb parked the car, exited, and approached his brother. "Greetings, my brother."

Adofo glared at him. "What brings you to Ghana?"

"I must talk with you."

"About what?"

"I think you know." He paused. "May I sit?"

His brother motioned to a chair beside him.

Jeb took a seat. "How are you doing, Adofo?"

"As well as can be."

Deep compassion for his brother overwhelmed Jeb. "Are you still grieving over Papa?"

Adofo's face grew taut. "I will never stop grieving over Papa."

"I am sorry that his passing has been so difficult for you."

Adofo gave him a questioning look. "Has it not been so for you as well?"

"Yes. But I think it struck you more forcefully because of your youth. It is one thing to have one's father for many years and quite another to have him for so few." Jeb placed a hand on Adofo's arm. "My heart goes out to you."

His brother drew back. "So, what is the purpose of your visit?"

"I have come to discuss the chieftaincy."

Adofo's jaw squared. "What about it?"

"I received a telegram from the tribal elders stating that they had chosen you as chief."

"So? What is that to you? Do you think I am not as capable as you of fulfilling the office?"

Jeb's muscles stiffened. He paused to choose his words carefully. "It is not a question of who is more capable. It is a question of integrity. Of honoring the rightful inheritance of the firstborn son of the outgoing chief. Of respecting the wishes and expectations of our father."

Adofo's face turned red. "But the fact of your primogeniture was a twist of fate."

"I don't think so. But it is a fact, nonetheless. And that fact cannot be denied without violating the integrity that Father instilled in us."

Adofo lowered his eyes and remained silent.

Jeb was direct. "Who put you up to it, Adofo? Was it Yafeu?"

"What makes you think that someone put me up to it? What if I volunteered myself as a candidate? Unlike you, I'm willing for the tribe to pick a wife for me." His voice dripped with sarcasm. "And she won't be white."

"I see. So, you're confirming that the reason I was not chosen is that my wife is white."

His brother shifted in his chair before offering a grudging response. "Yes."

"And what about Yafeu?"

"What about him?"

"Was he involved in your decision to seek the chieftaincy?"

"What makes you think he was involved?"

"He is the one who accused me of cowardice during the interview. He was looking for an excuse." Jeb lowered his voice. "I think he still grieves over the tragic death of his son."

Adofo nodded. "He has never gotten over it."

Jeb grew pensive. "Were it not for Yafeu's accusation, I could possibly have succeeded in swaying the elders regarding the racism issue."

Jeb's brother remained silent.

"Adofo, why did you allow yourself to be used as his pawn?"

Adofo straightened in his chair. "How dare you say that?"

"But that is exactly what you did, my brother!"

Adofo stood, his face flushed. "I am no man's pawn!"

"But don't you see that Yafeu used you to gain his own end?"

"What end?"

"Vengeance against me for not saving his son." Jeb sighed. "He could not admit to himself that he had never forgiven me. So, in order to hide his unforgiveness, in order to keep it from becoming obvious, he chose to use an innocent person who could easily be deceived. He used you to punish me."

Adofo's face grew red. "Are you insinuating that I am spineless?"

Jeb put a hand on his brother's shoulder. "No. You are not spineless. You have simply been misled. I want to show you the truth because it alone will set you free."

Adofo stared at Jeb and then shook his head as his anger deflated. "I can't believe it! I can't believe I was so deceived."

"Yafeu's way of punishing me for his son's death was to pit you against me by nominating you as chief. He knew that making you chief would deeply hurt me. And that hurt would be my punishment for Kofi's death."

"Well, *did* it hurt you?"

"At first, when Mama told me, yes. But then, as I began to see the motive behind it, I moved from anger toward you to compassion and forgiveness."

His shoulders sagging, Adofo turned away and walked to the edge of the veranda. He remained there for a long moment and then returned. "How can I be sure that what you are saying is the truth?"

"Look at it this way. A father loses his son in a tragic accident. He cannot live with the fact that his son died but his son's friend did not. The father tries to make sense of the insanity by casting blame. Casting blame is his way of punishing the only one who could have saved his son. Punishing the survivor makes his son's death bearable. Gives it sense. Helps the father to cope."

Adofo shook his head. "So, you are saying that Yafeu has never forgiven you for his son's death?"

"Yes. That is what I am saying, even though I was not responsible for his son's death. I did everything I could to save him." Jeb sighed, realizing even as he spoke the words that he fully believed them. "But when one refuses to forgive, one must punish."

Adofo sat down and put his face in his hands. "That is exactly what I wanted to do to you. Punish you."

"But, why, Adofo? What did I ever do to hurt you?"

"Yafeu baited me. He told me lies about you. He said that you did not love me but only loved yourself. He said that you thought you were better than I." The words choked in Adofo's throat. "He said that you needed to be brought down because of your pride." With tears in his eyes, he looked at Jeb. "And that he would help me to bring you down if I were willing."

Jeb's heart broke as he read the remorse in his brother's eyes.

Adofo lowered his voice to a whisper. "And I was willing, Jeb. I was willing." He broke down in tears. "It was not Yafeu's desire to become chief himself. It was his desire to deny you the chieftaincy. And I was a willing accomplice in his abominable scheme."

Jeb put his arm around Adofo. "I forgive you, my brother."

Jeb remained with Adofo for a long while. When they parted, Jeb had Adofo's word that he would refuse the offer to be chief on the grounds of familial integrity.

And his love for his brother Jeb.

* * * *

After her grand exit from the rental clerk's office, Tori headed straight for her class at the university. Although she hadn't rented an apartment, she was proud of herself for standing up for what was right.

But, if today's incident were any indication, she would have a rough time finding a place to live unless she rented it alone.

But that was out of the question.

Maybe the only solution was for her and Jeb to move to Ghana and live there. After repeated instances of being denied an apartment because she was white and Jeb was black, the stupidity of racism struck her with even more force. She could not allow it to go unchecked. Yet, what could she do to rid society of this curse?

Maybe she should focus her efforts on fighting racism by telling the world about Jesus Christ. And then letting His love put an end to that scourge for once and for all.

Tori reached the art building just as the previous class dismissed. Dozens of students stood in front of the building, chatting and laughing. As she approached the entrance, she caught sight of the student who had assaulted her. She cringed and hurried up the steps before he noticed her.

Once inside, she released the long breath she'd been holding. But then she stopped, angry at herself for having given in to fear. She had nothing to fear. She was in the right, on the side of truth. And truth always prevailed over the lie. Racism was a lie! No human being could confer worth, nor could any human being take away worth.

Then a thought struck Tori. Pop had said she was an accident. That was a lie, too! Pop had no authority to make that determination. Only God could make it. And God, by creating her, had determined that she was not an accident. That He wanted her.

That she was here *on* purpose and *for* a purpose.

A rush of joy flooded Tori's heart. Knowing the truth did, indeed, make one free.

She hurried toward the lecture hall. If only she could talk with Jeb. She had so much she wanted to share with him. So many questions to ask him.

He'd promised to send her a telegram as soon as he had any news. But all she could do was wait.

She arrived at the lecture hall a few minutes before class and found Susanna already in her seat.

"Hi, Susanna!" Tori sat down next to her.

"Hi." Susanna smiled. "Any news?"

"I think you should nominate me for an Academy Award."

Susanna laughed. "Why?"

"You should have seen my performance at the rental office."

Susanna turned toward Tori, a question twinkling in her eyes. "So, tell me."

Tori went on to explain about the question on the application regarding the race of the applicants.

"Isn't it illegal to ask that?"

"Yes, but I'm finding out that, apparently, *illegal* doesn't carry much weight among some landlords."

"So, what did you do?"

"I tore up the application right in front of the clerk's face."

"You didn't!"

"I most certainly did!"

"I'm sorry, Tori. This whole thing must be a nightmare for you."

"Worse than that."

"Well, I hope it will be over soon."

"I'm hoping so, too."

Just then the professor walked into the classroom to begin the class. Tori had a hard time concentrating. All she could think about was Jeb and how he was faring in Ghana. No news was good news, but still, it would be nice to know what was going on.

Until she did, she would postpone the search for an apartment. Why waste any more time until she knew for certain what was going on with Jeb? It might turn out they would live in Ghana and wouldn't need an apartment in Philadelphia after all.

Tori spent the rest of the afternoon in the library, putting the final touches on her master's thesis. To her great relief, other than the bibliography, the thesis was finished.

It was dark when she returned to Susanna's apartment.

Susanna greeted her excitedly. "A telegram came for you a little while ago."

Tori's heart leapt as Susanna handed it to her.

"Would you mind if I read this privately?"

Susanna smiled. "Of course not."

Tori took the telegram into her bedroom. With trembling hands, she tore it open and read.

> *Tori, my Beloved,*
>
> *Miss you desperately. Matters progressing well here. Reconciled with Mama and Adofo. Meeting set with Yafeu. Still awaiting final decision by tribe. Will keep you informed. I love you!*
> *Jeb.*

Tori's eyes welled up with tears. Jeb missed her desperately. Just as she missed him. Longing and desire for her husband overwhelmed her. Lord willing, they would soon be together again, never more to part.

Much relieved, Tori refolded the telegram and placed it in her purse. So far, things seemed to be going well on the Ghana side of their marriage. Perhaps Jeb would be home soon and all would go well on this side of the equation as well.

At least, she could hope so.

She sat down at her desk to compose a short, return message to Jeb, acknowledging receipt of his telegram. Tomorrow she would go to the Western Union office to send him her reply.

She hoped that instead of another telegram from Jeb, the next time she would receive Jeb himself in person.

* * * *

Now that his relationship with Adofo was reconciled, and now that Adofo had admitted he'd been wrong in wresting the chieftaincy from Jeb, Jeb focused on his meeting with Yafeu. If he could reach this man's heart, then the battle for the chieftaincy would be won.

But reaching him would be a challenge. Bitterness often lay hidden deep in the human heart, unwilling to emerge and be brought to the light. So it seemed with Yafeu.

Yet, with God all things were possible.

Yafeu had agreed to meet with Jeb and Adofo that evening at his home. Jeb whispered a prayer as he and Adofo drove down the winding dirt road to Yafeu's house. The large dwelling was situated in a secluded location at the northern edge of the village, a good distance from most of the other inhabitants. After Kofi died, Yafeu had isolated himself from the tribe and had limited his participation in village life primarily to his role as a tribal elder. Rarely was he seen associating with the other members of the tribe. To the chagrin of the members, he'd become a virtual recluse.

By the time Jeb and Adofo left, the sun had already set and had ushered in an indigo, star-studded sky, with a full moon that lit up the dirt road before them. As they passed neighboring farms, the sound of bleating goats filtered through the car's open windows, reminding Jeb of the many happy hours he'd spent as a child tending to the friendly creatures.

Jeb turned toward his brother. "Are you nervous?"

He nodded. "Yes."

"Do you know why?"

"Because I have been like a son to Yafeu, and I feel as though now I am about to betray him."

"I understand." Jeb paused. "But, in truth, it is he who betrayed you."

Adofo remained silent, his face toward the road in front of them.

"Are you having second thoughts about this meeting, Adofo?"

"No. I am convinced we are doing the right thing. But it is still difficult."

"Yes. Doing the right thing is often very difficult. But we must do it, nonetheless."

They reached Yafeu's house. A single light shone through the window.

Jeb parked the car in an open space in front. He got out of the car and walked toward the house.

Adofo followed close behind him.

The sound of katydids filled the night air. In the distance, a jackal howled.

As he climbed the steps to the front veranda, Jeb's stomach clenched. Something was wrong. He stopped, all of his senses on high alert.

The sense of foreboding intensified.

Adofo approached Jeb's side. Jeb extended his right arm to stop his brother from going any farther.

Adofo turned to him in alarm. "What's wrong?"

"I don't know. I just have a bad feeling about being here."

Jeb knocked on the door. But there was no answer. He knocked again. Still no answer. "I wonder if Yafeu is all right."

Adofo stepped forward. "Let me try the door. Yafeu often leaves it open."

Before Jeb could stop him, Adofo opened the front door and went inside.

Instantly, an explosion rocketed Adofo across the room. The house burst into flames, and a beam overhead fell across the entrance, blocking it.

The explosion had knocked out a large windowpane adjacent to the door. In an instant, Jeb jumped through the open window into the midst of the flames.

The room was ablaze. Through the flames and the smoke, Jeb could barely see Adofo lying on the floor.

There was no time to lose.

Jeb wrestled his way through the threatening flames, jumping over debris that had fallen into the room. He could barely breathe. Like a mushroom cloud, smoke billowed outward from the center of the room, blinding his path. The acrid stench of burning sulfur permeated the air, choking him as he struggled to reach his brother.

O God! Please let Adofo live! Please spare him, O God!

The thought of losing his brother was more than Jeb could bear. It had been Jeb's idea to talk with Yafeu. They'd come to his house at Jeb's instigation. Just as Kofi had agreed to go fishing at Jeb's instigation.

If Adofo died, would it be Jeb's fault?

No! Jeb refused to accept the devil's counterattack. It would be the fault of the person who set the bomb.

Jeb pressed on. The fire raged, illuminating Adofo's body lying motionless on the floor. Jeb leapt over a fallen beam and, stooping low, with blistered arms swept up his brother's body. Then, rising, Jeb turned toward the open window where he'd entered.

A large segment of roof had collapsed in front of it, blocking it.

How to escape this ravaging inferno before it killed them both?

Jeb's heart pounded fiercely against his chest. His eyes burned. His throat was parched. His muscles ached.

Would they make it out alive?

Which way to turn now? The fire raged on all sides. Jeb scanned the perimeter of the house, looking frantically for the best way of escape. Gasping desperately for air, he pushed through a tall bank of leaping flames toward a hole in the wall caused by the explosion. All the while, he did his best to keep the flames away from his brother.

Finally, he burst through to the outside of the house. Just then, several of the men of the village arrived. Among them was chief elder Siisi Odamtten.

"Let me help you, Jebuni!" Elder Siisi took Adofo's feet while Jeb supported his brother's shoulders. The two of them carried a badly injured Adofo to the car.

Jeb gently lay an unconscious Adofo on the back seat and then entered the driver's side. He shouted through the open window. "Elder Siisi, please fetch Mama and bring her to the hospital right away."

The chief elder nodded.

As Jeb pulled away, he again cried out to God to spare his brother's life.

Chapter 17

Lonely and homeless, Tori left the Western Union office and headed back to Susanna's apartment. Despite the brightness of the late afternoon, Tori's heart was dark and heavy. Not even the clown performing his antics for the children in front of a nearby candy store could cheer her. Numb with disappointment, she walked by them, her soul throbbing with her own personal pain.

In the telegram she'd just sent to Jeb a few moments earlier, she'd informed him of her failure to rent an apartment. She'd also told him how much she loved him and missed him.

But what was she going to do now? She couldn't stay with Susanna indefinitely. She had to find another job right away. Perhaps she and Jeb should move to a different part of the country?

But where?

Where would an interracial couple be accepted, let alone welcomed?

And if they found such a place, when should she and Jeb move?

Her muscles tense, she inhaled a deep breath. Who knew how long Jeb would remain in Ghana? And whether or not he'd be installed as chief?

Had the tribe changed its mind about Adofo? Had the elders reconsidered that the chieftaincy belonged to Jeb by virtue of his birth and his birthright?

Had they finally agreed to do him justice and make him their chief?

So many unanswered questions. So many nagging doubts.

Not knowing was difficult.

Tori boarded the bus to Susanna's apartment. The bus was more crowded than usual and every seat was filled. She stood with several other passengers in the aisle, holding on to a leather strap on the ceiling that prevented passengers from falling. Nervously, she scanned the passengers. Did anyone know her? Should she prepare for another insult? Another slur?

Another assault?

Her body grew rigid at the possibility.

The old bus lumbered through the city streets, hissing as it rocked from side to side with the weight of its human load. After a short ride, it left Tori off in front of Susanna's apartment building. Tori climbed the stairs to the second floor and entered the apartment. Susanna was still in class, so Tori had the place all to herself.

She went into her bedroom. Weary from it all, she sank onto her cot and rested her head in her hands. *Lord, where to now? I've reached the end of my rope.*

In her spirit, she heard the word *Wait.*

Wait? How could she simply wait without doing anything?

But over the years of walking with the Lord, she'd learned to recognize that still, small voice. Now she needed to trust it.

Even when it seemed that trusting it made no sense.

Even when it seemed that trusting it would only bring more challenges.

Even when it seemed that trusting it would lead to disaster.

Tori sighed. She'd lost virtually everything that mattered to her. Her relationship with her parents. Her reputation. Her job.

But she still had Anna and Sue.

And, of course, she had Jeb. Dear, precious Jeb. How she thanked God for him! The man to whom she'd willingly and gladly pledged to share the rest of her life. The man who'd taught her that freedom was not only a right but also a responsibility.

Tori lifted her head and looked out the window. The March morning shone bright and clear.

And so did the hope rising anew in her heart. What did it matter if her parents—and the whole world—rejected her? God would never reject her. What did it matter if her parents— and the whole world— misunderstood her? God understood her perfectly. What did it matter if she, Jeb, and their children were ostracized? The Lord would never leave them nor forsake them.

She rose and walked to the window. A cluster of tulips just outside the apartment building stood in early bloom. An old maple tree sported infant leaves, while a small birdbath in the center of the lawn welcomed a chirping robin. In the distance, the Schuylkill River flowed calm and serene under a cloudless, blue sky.

Tori could barely discern the park where she and Jeb had pledged their lifelong love to each other. Nothing would destroy that love because nothing could destroy true love. It endured all things. It believed all things. It hoped all things.

True love never failed.

* * * *

Jeb drove as fast as he could to the nearest hospital, located in the center of Sekondi. His own body burned by the fire at Yafeu's house, he worried more about Adofo lying unconscious in the back seat. Would his only brother survive? Mama could not bear losing another loved one so soon after Papa's death.

Nor could he.

Fear for his brother's life clawed at Jeb's insides. Anger clawed there, too. Who could have perpetrated such a crime? And why?

Was Yafeu capable of such a horrendous act? Or had he, too, been duped and targeted by someone else?

Jeb pulled into the emergency room entrance and got out of the car. He quickly summoned help. In short order, two attendants stood at the side of the car with a gurney. Carefully, they removed Adofo from the back seat and whisked him into the hospital.

Jeb followed after them.

As several physicians attended to Adofo in one room, another physician attended to Jeb in another room. The doctor cleaned and dressed Jeb's burns, told him to drink lots of water, and prescribed an antibiotic to prevent infection.

When Jeb had been taken care of, he joined Adofo. His brother lay on the gurney, surrounded by doctors and nurses. One nurse had started an IV, while another carefully tended to his wounds.

Jeb addressed the head doctor. "How is he?"

"Your brother is in very serious condition. We will have to keep him indefinitely in the intensive care unit."

Jeb drew in a deep breath, seeking courage to ask the question he needed to ask. "Will he make it?"

The doctor's gaze rested squarely on Jeb's. "I do not know. Burns of this degree often result in death." His voice was somber. "I pray that he will survive."

Jeb swallowed the lump that had lodged in his throat. "I pray that he will as well."

While an attendant wheeled his brother to the intensive care unit.

Another attendant entered the examining room to remove Adofo to the Intensive Care Unit. Jeb followed him, praying all the while.

Jeb and Mama spent the entire night praying at the hospital.

Early the next afternoon, chief elder Siisi returned to the hospital. He took Jeb aside. "I must speak with you and your mother."

Jeb ushered Mama into the waiting area where she took a seat. Jeb sat at her side while elder Siisi sat across from them.

He folded his hands on his lap. "We have learned that there has been foul play at Yafeu's house." He looked at Jeb. "Unfortunately, there was an attempt on your life."

Jeb furrowed his brows. "*My* life? Whatever for? And by whom?"

"By Yafeu himself."

Jeb leaned forward in his chair. "But why?"

The chief elder cleared his throat. "He has never forgiven you for the death of his son. Since then, he has been looking for a way to punish you."

"But he knew Adofo would be with me. What did my brother have to do with all of this?"

"Adofo was the means to an end. The end was you. Adofo was simply a gullible pawn in the hands of a master deceiver."

Jeb shook his head. His own brother had taken the brunt of the vengeance directed at Jeb.

Jeb addressed the chief elder. "How did you learn this?"

"When news of the explosion reached the village, we sent men to investigate. They found Yafeu hiding in a nearby barn. When they questioned him, he finally confessed everything, including his motive."

"But he was willing to destroy his own home to kill me?"

"His home meant nothing to him if he could use it to achieve his wicked ends."

Jeb shook his head. "I had bad feelings about Yafeu at my chieftaincy interview. I knew he did not want me to be chief."

"He did not. He wanted you to be voted out because of Kofi's death."

Jeb drew in a deep breath. "I did not perceive the depth of his bitterness toward me. All these years, he never showed his true feelings. He said he had forgiven me."

The elder paused. "Yafeu is a broken man."

Jeb nodded. "So, what is to be done with him?"

"That decision will likely be yours to make."

"Mine?"

"Yes, yours!"

"How so?"

"Given what has occurred, I called an emergency meeting of the elders this morning to discuss the current situation. I convinced them that you were wronged. Since you are already married, I also convinced them to allow the right of inheritance to override tradition. They agreed. We shall appoint you tomorrow as *pro tempore* chief and then hold the official installation ceremony in June, after you graduate."

Jeb's heart soared. "What about the interim period while I finish my studies? Who will lead the tribe during that time?"

"With your permission, I will be happy to serve as interim chief until your return."

Jeb nodded. "You have my permission."

Elder Siisi's eyes teared. "I owe you an apology, Jebuni. I, too, was deceived by Yafeu and am profoundly sorry. I am also sorry for opposing your marriage to the woman of your choice."

"I forgive you." Jeb rose and moved toward the elder.

Elder Siisi rose in return and the two men embraced.

* * * *

The day of Yafeu's trial dawned gray and bleak. Jeb rose at sun-up to prepare for the long day ahead of him. Having received the unanimous approval of the elders after the horrific ordeal with Yafeu, he'd been appointed chief *pro tempore* until the completion of his studies.

He entered the town hall followed by the council of elders. Today he would determine Yafeu's punishment for his crime against Jeb and Adofo.

Adofo was still in the intensive care unit. Although he remained in critical condition, he'd survived the initial trauma, and doctors had deemed his chances for recovery as quite good.

Thank the Lord! Jeb and Mama had prayed fervently for a miracle, and God had answered their prayer.

One by one, the elders took their seats in the town hall while Jeb took his place on his rightful stool, facing them. The day was hot and muggy, but Jeb perspired more from nervousness than from the oppressive heat.

Today he would face the man who'd blatantly accused him of cowardice in the accidental death of his son Kofi. The man who'd lied when he'd said he didn't hold Jeb responsible for the death of his son.

The man whose bitterness had inspired a crime that had nearly taken Jeb's brother's life and seriously compromised his own.

Jeb waited until every elder had sat down. He then took a deep breath and looked out over the council seated before him.

"We are here to decree a verdict on Yafeu Adomako. I call for the attendant to bring him before the stool."

Yafeu entered the room, accompanied by a prison guard assigned to him, and stood directly in front of Jeb, facing him.

The room grew silent as all eyes focused on Jeb. In his hands lay the fate of the man who'd nearly killed Jeb's brother and badly injured Jeb.

Jeb looked at Yafeu.

The old man's wrinkled face wore the strain of much suffering. His dark, deep-set eyes, void of light, held bitterness mingled with deep grief. His shoulders were stooped with the weight of long years of deceit.

Jeb addressed him. "Elder Yafeu, do you have anything to say of the vicious attack that occurred at your house a few days ago against my brother and myself?"

The old man lowered his eyes. "I am guilty of the explosion."

Whispers arose among the seated council of elders.

In a strong, firm voice, Jeb continued. "What motivated you to perpetrate such a horrendous crime?"

Yafeu hesitated.

Jeb read the internal struggle written on the old man's face.

Yafeu raised his gaze, resting it squarely on Jeb. "Vengeance. Vengeance alone."

Was the look in Yafeu's eyes one of remorse or one of defiance? Had he perpetrated the crime out of deep grief or bitter hatred?

If both, which motive dominated his crime?

The meaning of the look would determine the sentence.

"Did you commit the crime alone, or was there an accomplice?"

"Entirely alone. There were no accomplices."

Jeb prayed silently for wisdom and discernment. He sought only truth in his judgment, whatever that truth might be.

"Do you understand the full implications of your actions?"

Yafeu nodded. "Yes."

Jeb stood and walked in front of the stool.

The entire room of elders sat silently, awaiting Jeb's verdict.

Jeb stood before Yafeu, his heart moved by the sight of the broken man before him. "If you were in my position, what would you do?"

"I would declare the death sentence upon me."

Jeb nodded. "And the death sentence would be what you would deserve." He paused and moved closer to Yafeu.

The old man flinched, as though fearful of Jeb's striking him.

Compassion flooded Jeb. "But, by God's grace, you are not in my position."

All eyes were on Jeb.

He raised his arm, allowing the broad sleeve of his colorful royal garment to hang full beneath him. "And since you are not in my position, I choose to forgive you of your crime and to allow you to live."

A universal exhalation of long-held breath sounded in unison among the elders. The council broke out in loud chatter.

Jeb lifted his palms toward them to silence them and then turned again toward Yafeu. "But, lest you think that such a horrific crime should go unpunished, I order you to serve ten years of confinement in the regional prison. Perhaps, during that time, you will grow aware of the seriousness of your offense not only against your fellow man, but especially against God."

Yafeu's gaze remained hard. "I am not deserving of such grace."

"None of us is deserving of grace, Yafeu Adomako. Ponder that truth for the next ten years. Even at the end of that period, you will not have had enough time to plumb the fullness of its meaning."

Jeb rose and turned toward the prison guard who had brought Yafeu into the council room. "You may return him to his cell for transfer to the regional prison."

After Yafeu and the prison guard had left, Jeb turned toward the elders. "I thank you for your presence here today. I thank you for reconsidering my position among you and for agreeing to install me as your new chief at the completion of my studies. In my absence, I officially appoint Elder Siisi as *pro tempore* chief. I pledge myself to lead our tribe with righteousness, justice, and compassion. I declare myself to be your loyal servant from this moment forward."

The tribal elders cheered and then came forward to welcome their new chief.

"Now that this matter is settled, I will return to the States to finish my studies, to rejoin my bride, and, in a few short months, to bring her back to Ghana."

Chief elder Siisi spoke. "Chief Jebuni, we welcome you as our new chief. We will welcome your new bride as well."

Jeb's heart warmed. Not only had they accepted him as their new chief, but they had accepted Tori as well.

Elder Siisi continued. "The installation will take place in late June, immediately upon your return from the States."

Jeb smiled. He couldn't wait to share the news with Tori.

Chapter 18

Three months later …

The Ghanaian sun in late June shone like a golden jewel against a backdrop of brilliant blue. A light breeze blew through the palm trees, carrying with it the appetizing smell of frying salted fish.

All around Tori in the village square, *kagan* and *kidi* drums vibrated as gaily dressed women danced and clapped their hands to the beat of the *axatse*, the traditional gourd rattle, and the *gankogui*, the traditional two-tone iron bell.

The area buzzed with excitement in preparation for the official enstoolment of the tribe's new chief, Jebuni Kalitsi. Celebration filled the air.

Tori sat on the platform next to Jeb, her heart full of admiration, respect, and pride for her husband. At long last, after many obstacles and much suffering, his dream—and his duty— would be fulfilled. Today he would be installed as the tribe's new chief.

Her heart stirred. The journey to this day had been long and hard, but oh, so worth it. In the four weeks since she'd moved to Ghana, Tori had fallen in love with the country, its people, and its art. To her great relief, the tribe—and Jeb's mother—had welcomed her with open arms and accepted her as their "mama"—an honor she did not take lightly.

Tori held her breath as Chief Elder Siisi rose and came to the front of the large square. The music and dancing stopped as he held up the palm of his hand to silence the crowd.

Calling Jeb to stand before him, the chief elder led him in the oath of allegiance to the tribe.

Slowly, deliberately, Jeb's firm, clear voice resounded through the air as he repeated each word with deep conviction.

Tears welled up in Tori's eyes as Jeb pledged, with his hand on his father's Bible, to respect and protect his people at all times and to uphold their traditions of valor, courage, and moral rectitude.

After taking the chieftaincy oath of office, Jeb proceeded to the stool with great solemnity and dignity. The stool was rectangular in shape and made from the wood of the *sese* tree. It was carved with images from Jeb's family history and from tribal traditions. The chief's stool represented the binding of the tribe throughout history as an organic entity. It was the focal point of the life of the community. The stool spoke of the chief's position as the tribe's temporal and spiritual leader. As a Christian, Jeb's stool represented his dependence on God to guide him in his office as chief.

Everyone's gaze was upon Jeb as he sat down upon it.

The crowd erupted in wild cheers.

A lump formed in Tori's throat as she gazed upon her husband, seated on his tribal throne.

After a few moments, Jeb stood to bless his people. Then, after the blessings, the men of the tribe lifted Jeb onto their shoulders and, with much shouting, paraded him around the village square, shouting their solid approval of their new chief. The music and dancing resumed even more joyously and loudly than before.

As the men carrying Jeb stopped in front of Tori, Jeb's eyes locked onto hers.

Her heart thrilled as she read in his gaze his promise to love her all the days of her life. To be loyal and faithful to her.

To cherish her and care for her like no other.

After several moments of exalting their new chief, the men lowered Jeb to the ground. He returned to Tori's side on the platform, sat down, and took her hand in his.

She squeezed his hand and smiled. "You did it, Jeb!"

He shook his head. "No, dearest one. *We* did it. Together. With God's help."

She nodded. Yes. Jeb was right. With God's help, they'd done it together. Together they'd scaled the mountains of obstacles that had sought to prevent them from their destiny. Together, they'd prevailed against all odds and triumphed over evil through forgiveness.

A lump formed in Tori's throat. Together, they'd proven that love never fails.

Tori looked out upon the people before her. They were now her people. Her tribe.

Her family.

And it had come about through forgiveness.

Jeb had forgiven Yafeu for nearly killing Adofo and for injuring him. Jeb's mother had forgiven Jeb for marrying a white woman. The tribal elders had forgiven Jeb for choosing his own wife.

And Tori had forgiven her own father and mother for having rejected her.

Tori's life had become one of unbridled forgiveness. Predetermined forgiveness.

Pre-emptive forgiveness.

What did Jesus call it? Forgiving seventy times seven? Which meant forgiving endlessly, no matter how many times one was insulted or offended or assaulted or abused. No matter how many times one was hurt or suppressed or slandered or mocked.

Yes, she would forgive. Forgiveness would be her *modus operandi*. Her M.O., as Jeb would call it.

Forgiveness was love in action. And love was the key to life.

Jeb turned toward her. "May I invite my bride to dance with the chief?"

Tori's body tensed and her face grew hot. "But I don't know your dances."

Jeb laughed. "No problem. I will teach you."

Tori's heart raced as Jeb took her hand and led her off the platform into the center of the square. Her stomach clenched with panic as she realized that all eyes were upon her.

The chief's bride.

Would she prove worthy of him?

Or would she bring him ridicule?

Clinging to Jeb's hand, she searched his eyes for encouragement. His smile of approval was all that she needed.

Following his instructions—and watching his feet—she began to dance.

Holding Tori's hand, Jeb demonstrated a few basic steps of a Ghanaian dance.

Tori followed suit.

Jeb's eyes never left hers.

The more she danced, the freer she felt.

Soon she was dancing like a native Ghanaian.

The people roared with delight. They encouraged her. Accepted her. Loved her with passion.

No longer did it matter that Pop had rejected her. That he'd considered her an accident.

No. Jeb's people welcomed her. Loved her for who she was. White skin and all.

Soon the entire tribe was dancing with them. Encouraging Tori in her efforts. Approving of her.

Accepting her.

Her heart rang with joy. These were her people. Her heart was one with theirs.

Not because of skin color.
But because of love.
The love that came from Christ.
The only love that could make people of all nations one.

EPILOGUE

Five years later …

"Vincent Jebuni Kalitsi! Come here right now!"

Tori suppressed a smile as she called to her four-year-old son, named after her father.

He laughed as he ran away from her, inviting her into a teasing chase.

Joining him in laughter, Tori lunged toward him, gathered him up into her arms, and spun him around in the air. Her heart soared as she looked into the beautiful eyes of her precious little boy. How she loved him! With his round, cherub face and his curly, honey-colored hair. He looked just like Jeb. The same deep-set eyes. The same strong nose. The same bright smile.

She gently lowered Vincent to the ground and took his hand. "Let's go see Nonno and Nonna."

Vincent let go of her hand and ran straight to Tori's father, seated in a bamboo rocking chair next to Tori's mother on the veranda of Jeb and Tori's home in Ghana.

"Nonno! Nonno!" Vincent ran straight into his grandfather's open arms.

"Hey, Vinnie!" Vince Pendola picked up his grandson and held him close.

The little boy wrapped his arms around his grandfather's neck.

Tori's heart filled, as a tear rolled down her father's cheek. How close he'd come to missing this precious moment, and all the other precious moments he'd experienced with her and his grandchildren since he'd decided to let go of his prejudice. How thankful she was that he'd changed his thinking! It was the miracle she and Jeb had prayed for for so long.

"Nonno, pick me up, too!" Tori's two-year-old daughter, Dela, stood before her grandfather, her little arms outstretched toward him.

Smiling broadly, Tori's father shifted Vinnie to one knee and then placed his little granddaughter on his other knee. "There! Both of my grandchildren are on my knees. What shall we do now?"

"Let's play horsey!" Vinnie started galloping on his grandfather's left knee, and Dela followed suit on his right knee. Soon the three of them were heading to imaginary places, laughing all the way.

Tears welled up in Tori's eyes as well. Who would have ever thought—five long years ago—that one day her father and mother would be sitting on her veranda in Ghana, doting over their grandchildren?

Jeb joined them on the veranda, his usual broad smile flashing.

Tori's heart still fluttered at the sight of her handsome husband. Five years of marriage had only made their love stronger and deeper.

Jeb laughed. "Whoa! Look at those horses go!"

"Papa, look!" Vincent's voice filled the air. "We're riding with Nonno to the stars!"

Jeb smiled and pointed a warning finger at Vincent. "Just be sure you're back in time for dinner."

Tori rose. "Speaking of dinner, it's time for me to start cooking."

"Let me help you." Tori's mother followed her into the house.

Once in the kitchen, Tori gave her mother a hug. "You have no idea how happy I am to have you and Pop here. This is a dream come true for me."

"And for me, too." Her mother paused, a serious look on her face. "Tori, there is so much for which your father and I need to ask your forgiveness. Since we've come to Christ, we see life and the world so differently." She placed her arm around Tori's shoulders. "And we have you and Jeb to thank for that. Had you not remained true to your beliefs and married Jeb, we may never have seen racism for what it is. An ugly blot on the human soul. A divider of people. A destroyer of love."

Mom leaned against the countertop and folded her hands in front of her. "When you told us that we had a grandson, we started thinking and asking ourselves some hard questions. Did we want our prejudice to keep us from enjoying the beautiful family God had given us? Were we willing to give that up because of our own foolish pride?"

"So, when did you and Pop change your mind?"

"During a long conversation with Anna."

Dear, sweet Anna! Tori couldn't wait for her sister to join them in a few days.

"What did Anna say that influenced you?"

"She asked us if we wanted to grow old with bitter, unforgiving hearts that kept us alienated from our family, or did we want to grow old with loving, forgiving hearts that would fill our latter years with the joys of happy family relationships. And grandchildren! She told us the choice was ours."

Tori listened attentively.

"And Anna was right. The choice *was* ours." Mom sighed. "So, your father and I decided to put aside all anger, bitterness, and pride. We decided to do things God's way." Tears filled Mom's eyes. "And what you see here today is the result."

Tori gave her mother a tight hug. "Oh, Mom! I love you so much!"

"And I love you, too, my precious Tori."

Pop strode into the kitchen. "So, what's for dinner?" He looked at Tori and Mom. "You mean you haven't started cooking yet?"

Mom took his arm. "We had something more important to do first."

"What's more important than food?" Pop joked.

"There's food for the body and there's food for the soul. Tori and I just had an appetizer of food for the soul. Now we'll prepare food for the body."

"And what will that be?"

Tori smiled. "Your favorite, Pop. Spaghetti and meatballs!"

"In Africa?"

"Why, of course!" Tori laughed. "Would you believe that spaghetti and meatballs is Jeb's favorite dish?"

Just then Jeb walked into the kitchen. "Did I hear my name?"

Tori took his arm. "Yes. I just told Pop that spaghetti and meatballs is your favorite dish."

Pop placed a hand on Jeb's shoulder and smiled. "That's my son-in-law. A man after my own heart—and stomach! You make me proud!"

Joy exploded in Tori's heart. Hearing Pop's words to Jeb was worth all the suffering, all the misunderstanding, and all the rejection of the past.

Yes, love had a price. And Love Himself, the Lord Jesus Christ, had paid that price.

She and Jeb had committed to spending their lives proclaiming that love.

The love that alone could redeem, reconcile, and restore.

THE END

QUESTIONS FOR GROUP DISCUSSION

NOTE: These questions may be used in a variety of ways, including book club or reading-group discussions, and in Bible-study groups dealing with the topics of racism, prejudice, rejection, and other topics related to division among human beings.

1. Tori struggled with rejection issues as a result of not being wanted by her parents, especially her father. Have you ever struggled with rejection from your parents or another loved one? How did you handle it? True freedom comes when we grasp the truth that God will never reject us. He accepts us as we are because He created us. Are you looking to God to reveal to you your true identity, or are you looking to your family, friends, or the world?

2. Bitterness has many roots. Jeb and Yafeu struggled with bitterness for different reasons. Tori's parents were consumed with bitterness against blacks. How did each of these characters handle bitterness? What is God's way of handling bitterness? What are some of the consequences of not handling bitterness God's way?

3. Jeb was betrayed by his own brother. Have you ever been betrayed? How did you feel? How did you respond? Betrayal often comes from those we love most. How does forgiveness remove the sting of betrayal?

4. Why do you think racism exists? Scripture teaches us that all of us descend from Adam and Eve. So, all of us have the same original parents. Why, then, would skin color matter? We must realize that we have an enemy named Satan. His goal is to steal, kill, and destroy. He desires division in families, churches, and ethnic groups. What can you do to foster unity, reconciliation, and understanding in those groups where you notice division?

5. What does Tori and Jeb's relationship show about the power of love to overcome racism? Their love was beyond romantic. It was *agape* love—the true love of God. Are you loving with *agape* love? The thirteenth chapter of 1 Corinthians describes *agape* love. Is there an area of *agape* love in which you need to improve? If so, how are you going to change your behavior?

AUTHOR'S NOTE

The seed for this story was planted in the year 1994 when the Holy Spirit began to stir my heart regarding the problem of racism. Up until then, I had not thought much about prejudice, although I'd personally been a victim of it. Back in the seventies, I'd applied for a job as a teacher of Italian. At that time, I had recently earned the Master of Arts degree in Italian Language and Literature. Moreover, Italian was my mother tongue and the first language I learned as a child. So, I was qualified to teach the language.

When I applied for the job, however, I was told to "go back to your own people." The person hiring held prejudice against Italians, and for that reason, he turned me away. Too stunned to say anything, I walked away. In those days, there was little if any recourse regarding discrimination policies in hiring. Had the situation occurred today, I would have handled it quite differently.

Perhaps it was that experience that set me on the road to understand racial prejudice. Over the years, I have come to this conclusion: There is only one race, and that race is the human race. Moreover, racism is a problem that can be solved only by a radical transformation in the human heart. And that radical transformation can occur only by accepting Jesus Christ as one's Savior and Lord.

If you have not yet accepted Christ as your Savior and Lord, I urge you to do so now. He alone is the answer to the problem of racism and to every other problem you will ever face.

ACKNOWLEDGMENTS

Books are the fruit of the efforts of far more people than simply the author. Books are born from the combined efforts of many people with multiple talents, all of whom pool their resources to produce works worthy of readers. Such, I trust, is the case with this novel you are holding in your hands.

Above all, I would like to thank God my Father in Heaven for giving me the idea for this book. He is the Giver of every good gift. This story is a gift from His heart to mine. Thank You, Father, for entrusting me with Your gift. I worship You!

I would like to thank my Lord and Savior, Jesus Christ, for sustaining me as I wrote this book. Lord Jesus, You are the Awesome Redeemer, the Reconciler, and the Restorer. Thank You for redeeming me from sin and sickness, for reconciling me to the Father, and for restoring me to wholeness. I love You!

I would like to thank You, Holy Spirit, my precious Guide and Counselor, as You unfolded to me this story of Your heart. I could feel Your Presence hovering over me as I wrote. Thank You for guiding me on this creative journey and pointing me in the direction of Your choosing. I adore You!

Heartfelt thanks are also due to my superstar husband Dom who helped me with the grocery shopping, the cooking, and the cleaning as I worked tirelessly "in the zone." He also helped me with the historical research that serves as the background for this novel and did an outstanding, amazing job of proofreading and editing the manuscript.

Deep and loving thanks to my precious daughters, Dr. Lia Diorio Gerken and Gina Diorio, who prayed me through the tough times. I am so honored to be your Mom. You are the best!

Heartfelt thanks go to my awesome Prayer Team—you know who you are!—who stood beside me every step of the way, upholding me through the many trials that presented themselves during the writing of this book. Love and blessings to you!

A very special debt of gratitude goes to my dear friend and sister in Christ, Joan Anderson Gangwer, for faithfully upholding me in prayer through the writing of this book. Joan, you are a blessing!

A special debt of gratitude goes to my dear friend, the late Sujen Croman, whose faithful prayers and encouragement sustained me during difficult times of writing.

A special thanks to my editor, Leslie Peterson, whose insightful comments made this story so much stronger because of her editorial skills.

A big Italian hug to my fabulous book designer, Lisa Vento Hainline, with whom the Lord supernaturally connected me and who has become a dear and precious friend.

Last, but certainly not least, sincere thanks to my precious readers. Without you, this book would have no home. May its home be your heart. May it bless you and touch the deepest places within you with the redemptive, reconciling, and restorative love of Jesus Christ!

SOCIAL MEDIA SITES

You will find Dr. MaryAnn on the following social media sites:

Websites: www.maryanndiorio.com and www.maryanndancioministries.com

Amazon Author Central: www.amazon.com/author/maryanndiorio

Authors Den: www.authorsden.com/maryanndiorio

BlogTalk Radio: www.blogtalkradio.com/drmaryanndiorio

BookBub.com: www.bookbub.com/authors/maryann-diorio

Christian Authors Network (CAN): christianauthorsnetwork.com/mary-ann-diorio/

Facebook: www.facebook.com/DrMaryAnnDiorio

Goodreads: www.goodreads.com/author/show/6592603

Instagram: www.instagram.com/drmaryanndiorio/

Library Thing: www.librarything.com/profile/drmaryanndiorio

LinkedIn: www.linkedin.com/in/maryann-diorio-phd-dminmfa-99924513/

Pinterest: www.pinterest.com/drmaryanndiorio/

Twitter: twitter.com/@DrMaryAnnDiorio

Vimeo: vimeo.com/user46487508

YouTube: www.youtube.com/user/drmaryanndiorio/

About the Author

Dr. MaryAnn Diorio is a widely published award-wining author of fiction for both children and adults. Her passion is to proclaim truth through fiction because only truth will set people free (John 8:32).

A widely published author of nonfiction as well, MaryAnn responded to God's call a few years ago to write fiction and has since published three novels, *The Madonna of Pisano*, *A Sicilian Farewell*, and *Return to Bella Terra*, all part of *The Italian Chronicles Trilogy*. She has also published two novellas, *A Christmas Homecoming* and *Surrender to Love*, as well as six children's books: *Who Is Jesus?*, *Toby Too Small*, *Candle Love*, *Do Angels Ride Ponies?*, *The Dandelion Patch*, and *Poems for Wee Ones*.

MaryAnn holds the Doctor of Philosophy (PhD) degree and the Master of Philosophy (MPhil) degree in French and Comparative Literature from the University of Kansas, the

Master of Arts (MA) degree in Italian Language and Literature from Middlebury College/University of Florence, Italy, the Master of Fine Arts (MFA) degree in Writing Popular Fiction from Seton Hill University, and the Bachelor of Arts (BA) degree in French from Immaculata University. She is also a Licensed Minister and a Certified Life Coach.

MaryAnn lives in New Jersey with her husband Dominic, a retired physician. They are blessed with two amazing adult daughters, a very smart son-in-law, and six rambunctious grandchildren. In her spare time, MaryAnn loves to read, paint, and make up silly songs with her grandchildren.

MaryAnn hopes her stories will entertain and point readers to Jesus Christ, the Truth Who alone can set them free.

How to Live Forever

Eternal life is a free gift offered by God to anyone who chooses to accept it. All it takes is a sincere sorrow for your sins (contrition) and a quality decision to turn away from your sins (repentance) and begin living for God. In John 3:3 KJV, Jesus said, "Except a man be born again, he cannot see the kingdom of God." What does it mean to be "born again"? Simply put, it means to be restored to fellowship with God.

Man is made up of three parts: spirit, soul, and body (1 Thessalonians 5:23 KJV). Your spirit is who you really are; your soul comprises your mind, your will, and your emotions; and your body is the housing for your spirit and your soul. You could call your body your "earth suit."

When we are born into this world, we are born with a spirit that is separated from God. As a result, it is a spirit without life, because God alone is the Source of life. You may have heard this condition referred to as "original sin." Why is every human being born with a spirit separated from God? Because of the sin of Adam, our first parent.

I used to wonder why I had to suffer because of Adam's sin. After all, I complained, I wasn't even there when he and Eve ate the apple! Yet, as I began to understand spiritual matters, I began to see that I was there just as a man and woman's children, grandchildren, great-grandchildren, and so on, are in the body of the man and woman in seed form before those descendants are actually born. In other words, in my children there is already the seed for their future children. In their future children will be the seed of their future children, and so on.

Now, as a parent, I can pass on to my children only what I am and what I possess. For example, I can pass on to my children only my own genetic makeup. The same is true of my husband. I possess no other genetic makeup to pass on to them. And the same was true with Adam. Because he disobeyed God, his fellowship with God was broken. Therefore, his spirit died because it was severed from God. As a result, he could pass on to his descendants only a dead spirit—a sinful spirit, separated from God. And Adam's children could pass on to their children only a dead, sinful spirit. And so on, all the way down to you and me.

We said earlier that your spirit is the real you—who you really are. So what does it mean when our spirit is separated from God? It means that unless we are somehow reconciled to God, we will be eternally separated from him. That is what hell is: a place of real torment resulting from eternal separation from God.

Now God is a holy God, and He will not tolerate sin in His presence. At the same time, He is a loving God. Indeed, He *is* Love! And because He loves you so much, He wanted to restore the broken relationship between you and Himself. He wanted to restore you to that glorious position of walking and talking with Him and enjoying the fullness of His blessings.

But there was a problem. Because God is infinite, only an infinite being could satisfy the price of man's offense against God. At the same time, because man committed the offense, there had to be Someone who would also be able to represent man in paying this price. In other words, there had to be a being who was both God and man in order that the price for sin could be paid.

Since God knew there was nothing man could do on his own to pay the price for his sin, God took the initiative. In the writings of John the Apostle, we learn that "God so loved the world, that he gave his only begotten Son, that whosoever believeth in him should not perish, but have everlasting life" (John 3: 16 KJV).

What glorious good news! God loved you so much that He sent His one and only Son, Jesus Christ, to take the rap for your sins. Imagine that! Would you give your son to go to the electric chair for someone else? Well, that's exactly what God did! The cross was the electric chair of Christ's day, and God gave His own Son, Jesus Christ, to go to the Cross for you!

In dying on the Cross for you, and in rising from the dead three days later, Jesus paid the price for your sins and repaired the breach between you and God the Father. Jesus restored the broken relationship between man and God. He provided mankind with the gift of eternal life.

So what does all of this mean for you? It means that if you accept Christ's gift of eternal life, you will be "born again." In other words, God will replace your dead spirit with a spirit filled with His life. "Therefore if any man be in Christ, he is a new creature: old things are passed away; behold, all things are become new" (2 Corinthians 5: 17 KJV).

If I offer you a gift, it is not yours until you choose to take it. The same is true with the gift of eternal life. Until you choose to take it, it is not yours. In order for you to be born again, you must reach out and take the gift of eternal life that Jesus is offering you now. Here is how to receive it:

"Lord Jesus, I come to You now just as I am—broken, bruised, and empty inside. I've made a mess of my life, and I need You to fix it. Please forgive me of all of my sins. I accept You now as my personal Savior and as the Lord of my life. Thank You for dying for me so that I might live. As I give You my life, I trust that You will make of me all that You've created me to be. Amen."

If you prayed this prayer, please write to me to let me know. I will send you some information to help you get started in your Christian walk. Also, I encourage you to do three important things:

1. Get yourself a Bible, and begin reading it, starting with the Gospel of John.
2. Find yourself a good church that preaches the full Gospel. Ask God to lead you to a church where you can learn His righteous ways of thinking and living.
3. Set aside a time every day for prayer. Prayer is simply talking to God as you would to your best friend.

I congratulate you on making the life-changing decision to accept Jesus Christ! It is the most important decision of your life. Mark down this date because it is the date of your spiritual birthday. Be assured of my prayers for you as you grow in your Christian walk. God bless you!

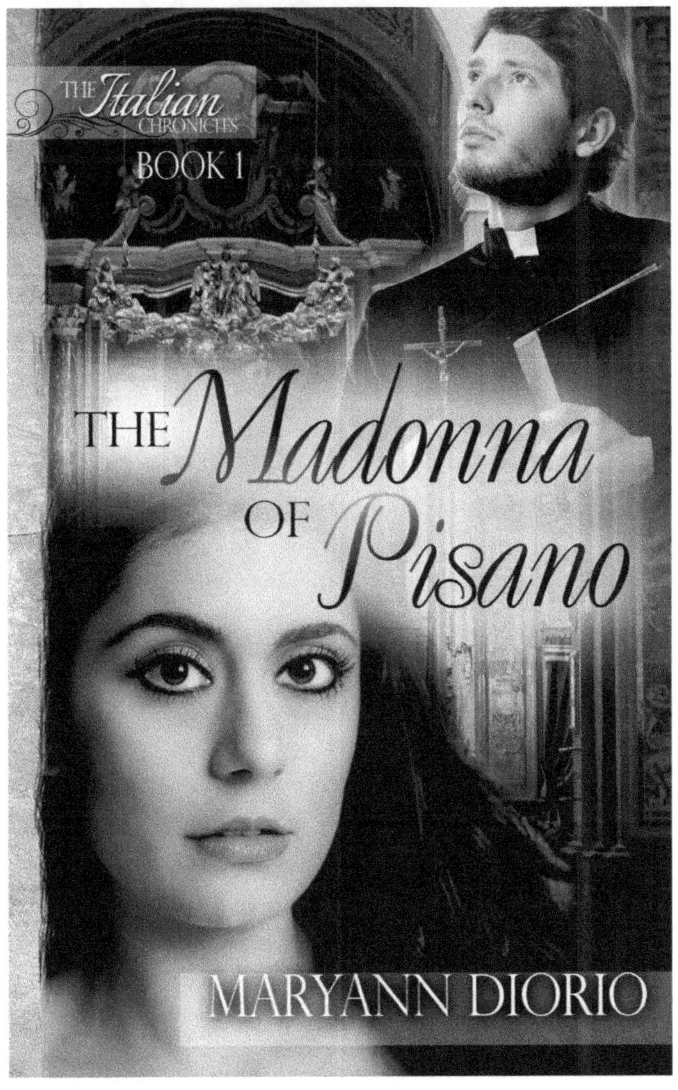
THE Italian
CHRONICLES
BOOK 1
THE Madonna
OF Pisano
MARYANN DIORIO

A young woman, a new land, and a dream
that threatens to destroy her, her marriage, and her family...

Return to Bella Terra
Book Three in
The Italian Chronicles Series

THE Italian CHRONICLES
BOOK 3
RETURN TO
Bella Terra
MARYANN DIORIO

*A mother, her son, and the man
who threatens to come between them …*

Other Books by Dr. MaryAnn Diorio